TEA LEAVES & TROUBLED SPIRITS

CONFESSIONS OF A CLOSET MEDIUM BOOK 6

NYX HALLIWELL

Beach
Path
Publishing

Tea Leaves & Troubled Spirits, Confessions of a Closet Medium, Book 6

© 2022 Nyx Halliwell

Print ISBN: 978-1-948686-75-4

Cover Art by Fanderclai Design **www.fanderclai.com**

Formatting by Beach Path Publishing, LLC

ONE

"This is a new low, even for me." I huddle in the corner, tightening my jacket. I wish I'd brought a heavier one. I should have known it would be cold, but I didn't expect the tundra.

"It's so exciting," my young companion says. Lia's black corkscrews are tamed under a head wrap. She fiddles with a machine she calls a ghost box, checking lights and dials. Her fingerless gloves were made by her grandmother, and a few reflective threads in the knitted flowers attached to the tops catch the soft glow from the exit sign over the door. While it's a balmy August night outside, we're dressed like it's December. In North Dakota. "I can't believe I'm ghost hunting in a morgue!"

"We're not *hunting* anything." Not technically. I do hope we can wrap this up quickly. *Nothing better than being in a hospital morgue at midnight*—said no psychic medium ever. "We're hoping the earthbound spirit who's been terrorizing the coroner and attendants makes an appearance. That's all. Then I can cross him to the afterlife."

The blanket we're sitting on is spread out as if we're on a picnic. The girl has an assortment of items placed on it. "You believe Dr. Ernestine about the hauntings?"

"I wouldn't be here if I didn't."

Lia pulls out her phone and taps the screen. "Can I get that on record for my vlog?"

Ophelia Chen works for me as my bookkeeper, an internship that is helpful to both of us. She is fascinated with the dead, and while I can see and hear them, I wish I couldn't. "This is not going on your vlog, Lia."

"But you said—"

"That I need help in case the ghost shows up." I pat my bag of tools lying at my feet. "Remember what I told you to do if he appears?"

She deflates and says in a monotone voice, "Sprinkle a line of salt around him. Light the sage bundle. Keep the holy water and iron cross ready in case he tries to reanimate a corpse."

"And?"

"Stay out of the way."

The poor medical examiner, Dr. Latimer, has turned gray overnight with the recent happenings in this room. I would too if a dead body sat up on the metal table while I was performing an autopsy and waved at me. Yes, according to Dr. Ernestine, who hired me for this gig, our ghost has the ability to inhabit a cadaver and make it move. Talk about a horror show. No wonder the head of the coroner's office for a decade is considering early retirement. "If we're successful, you can write up the basic details of the experience, okay? No names or specifics, but at least you'll have a story."

She recovers, looking hopeful. "Can I interview you?"

Keeping my mediumship skills under wraps is challenging, so broadcasting them to the world is definitely off the menu. "Absolutely not."

Her shoulders sink and she casts her gaze to the floor. "The team will be so disappointed."

Her "team" of ghost-hunting friends are a motley collection of kids who don't fit the norm in our small southern town of Thornhollow. The four of them also make up the AV and math clubs at the high school. Lia pretended there were far more in each of her extra-curricular classes, but when Mrs. Cook, the teacher in charge of the interns, spoke with me, she filled me in on the limited and somewhat "unhealthy" dependency they have on each other. Her words, not mine. Mrs. Cook stressed that being employed by me could expand Lia's social network, as well as her work experience.

Obviously, Mrs. Cook is unaware of my, *ahem*, abilities. "Your friends will be in awe of the fact you spent time in the morgue with a bunch of dead bodies."

"True!" Snagging her handheld camcorder she's tweaked to capture paranormal phenomena, she checks the battery. With infrared night vision, I wonder how long it took her to save up for it. "Ghosts typically manifest at night because they feed on our psychic energy while we're sleeping, right?"

I refrain from rolling my eyes. "I've seen plenty of them during the day."

"But that's why we're here now, because the odds are better to interact with this guy."

"Dr. Latimer and the nightshift employees have witnessed his exploits around midnight when it happens. Stands to reason this is the optimum time to reach him."

"Awesome." She trades the camcorder for her headlight, snugging the adjustable straps tighter on her skull and looking like she's about to enter a mine. She's explained that this is for hands-free "hunting," so she can grab her EMF device or recorder instantly. "It's the place to be, then. A hot spot."

Yet, we haven't seen or heard a thing. I'm grateful it's quiet from the standpoint that there isn't a body waiting for an autopsy, nor any attendants to distract us. "It's awfully cold for a hot spot."

"And getting colder." She points to another device that measures ambient room temperature and records video as well. "The FLIR shows we just dropped five degrees!"

Which is a sign of paranormal activity. Each of us scans the room. A series of metal doors line the wall across from us. I raise a hand to check if I feel air movement. "Did the AC kick on?"

The EMF's lights go from green to red. Ghosts need a lot of energy to manifest, and the electromagnetic field is a by-product of that. Red is a whopping high amount. "Nope!" She's giddy. "It must be him."

I get to my feet, sweeping my gaze around the shadows and holding my breath. Neither Ernestine nor Latimer have any idea who our ghost is, which makes it harder for me to know how to get him to cross, but I'm prepared. At least, as much as one can be when dealing with an unruly earth-bound spirit.

Lia grabs her camera and turns on her ghost box. "Come to mama," she says.

I hush her, listening. Outside, I hear the approach of a siren—most likely an ambulance. I try to tune it out and concentrate on noises close by. The quiet hum of a generator is all I hear, probably keeping the bodies behind the metal doors cool. I shiver thinking about them.

The hospital itself has a few resident spirits, most of which I've left alone when visiting friends. If they're attached to this plane and haven't crossed over, they have unfinished business. Some need to know a loved one who's still alive is okay. Others want closure about their death, especially if it was unexpected or violent.

The temperature drops again and my breath becomes visible. "Hello," I say, assuming our guest of honor has arrived. "I'm Ava, and I'm here to help you. I can see and hear spirits, so let's chat. What's your name?"

The siren draws nearer. Lia begins to circle the room. "I'm Lia," she adds with a wave.

Silence from the ghost, but the pounding of running feet can be heard overhead. The morgue is under the emergency clinic entrance, and has been here since the place was built after the Civil War.

"Can you make yourself visible?" While I typically spend my days as a party planner and wedding gown designer, I haven't had a break from helping ghosts since... well, I died for a few minutes and Logan, my now husband, brought me back to life last fall. Our first kiss was actually CPR. I'd give my left foot to go home and crawl into bed with him right now. "I'd love to hear your story about how you died and why you're hanging around"—why would anyone want to haunt a morgue?—"here."

Lia sidles up on my right, her palm-sized camera adding a greenish glow to the room with its night vision light. "You're so polite."

"You can thank my mother for that." The ambulance arrives, its siren cutting off abruptly. "Please," I say to the ghost, "at least tell us your name." *So I can get on with this.*

Above us, the commotion of the person in distress being

delivered to the ER continues. It wasn't long ago I was in that part of the hospital, bringing my friend and office manager, Rosie, in to have her second child. I send up a little prayer for whoever is in need.

The handles on the metal lockers across from us rattle, starting at one end and racing to the other. It's as if our ghost is playing an instrument. I'm just glad he can't seem to actually open them.

Lia's eyes go wide and she glances at me with a delighted grin, still making sure her camera is recording the activity. "Whoa."

"You're quite powerful," I tell our guest of honor. Appealing to his ego might get him to show himself. "Most spirits can't make things move."

A blast of frigid air hits my face. "Boo!"

Startled, I jump back. I know he's a jokester, yet didn't anticipate he'd try to scare me. He's still invisible, but at least I can hear him. "Funny. What's your name?"

"Avenger," he says, and he flicks my ponytail.

I whip around, but still can't see him. "I would appreciate you acting more mature. Face me and tell me your name."

"Clean the wax from your ears! I did!"

Lia can't hear him, but her EMF device is going crazy with lights and a whirring sound. "What is he saying?"

"That his name is Avenger."

"Like the superheroes?"

I shrug, disappointed this appears to be about revenge. Those are the tough ones. "Did someone hurt you, Avenger?" I cringe at using the ridiculous name.

There's a sneer in his voice as he sweeps past me. "He cut me up and sold me off."

Unsure of how to respond, I consider what that means. "Who did?"

There's no reply this time. Instead, he somehow manages to shove my tools across the floor. "Get out and leave me alone!"

I pick up the bag and grab the sage bundle. "Afraid I can't do that. Your actions are scaring people and disrespecting the dead who end up on the table." I light the bundle and blow out the flame so it smokes. I close my eyes and imagine a beautiful doorway leading to the afterlife. "Do you see the white light?"

He smacks my hand, causing me to drop the sage. "That stuff won't work on me!"

Why do we always have to do this the hard way? I retrieve my tool. "You need to cross over. What's done is done and you can't change that. I'm sorry, but you're dead, and you need to move on. Go to the light."

He cusses at me, and I'm glad Lia can't hear his suggestion of what I should do to myself.

Being polite rarely works. I feel sorry for most of them, but when they act like this, it's a challenge to hold my tongue and not let my temper get the best of me. I take a deep breath and count to ten. Then, "How can I help you resolve your anger?"

The exterior door down the hall opens and closes. The squeak of sneakers on linoleum follows, along with the sounds of someone whistling.

Before I can regroup, I see a man in a lab coat pushing a gurney with a body on it. A white blanket covers the person. He bangs into the metal swinging doors and flips on the bright overhead lights.

"Dude," Lia complains, blinking. She checks her camera and makes an adjustment. "We're working here."

The skinny young man with acne and a pitiful beard looks startled. "What the...?"

The room instantly becomes warmer. The ghost is gone. I tamp out the smoking sage, praying with all my might it worked to get rid of him, but I know better. The angrier they are, the more power they have, and that makes them harder to get rid of.

I motion at Lia to pack up as I eye the covered body on the gurney. "We have permission from Dr. Ernestine for a..."

"Documentary," Lia supplies, pulling off her headlamp.

"On the morgue?" the fellow asks.

"It's a historical site," I tell him, and Lia nods. "Goes back to the Civil War."

For whatever reason, this seems to legitimize us and he relaxes. "My dad is a reenactment buff."

"We'll get out of your way." I point to his charge. "Looks like you've got work to do."

He wheels the cart toward the table in the center. "Suicide," he tells me. "A jumper."

With our gear in tow, I guide Lia toward the exit. We've almost made it out when the ghost of the recently deceased pops into view right in front of me. "What happened?" He floats a few inches above the floor, eyes wide. "Why am I here?"

I cover my shock by clearing my throat. "What a shame," I say to the attendant.

The ghost stares at his body, not seeming to comprehend. Lia and I make our getaway, and as I'd hoped, the spirit follows to a quiet place in the hall. "You're dead," I murmur to him. "I'm sorry."

Lia gives me an odd look. "Avenger?"

"No." I shake my head. "The man they just brought in."

"I would never take my own life," he insists. "Never. I don't understand."

He vanishes and I let out my breath. "He's gone now," I say to Lia. "Let's go."

We make it upstairs to the hospital's main doors when a voice stops me. "Ava?"

I glance over and see two men at the ER desk. Two *living* men. "Brax? Rhys? What are you guys doing here?"

Brax LaFleur, my best friend in the world, towers over me. "There's been an accident at the B&B."

Rhys, who's been crying, rushes to hug me. "Our guest jumped out the third story window!"

TWO

I steer them toward the main waiting area to the right of the sliding doors of the entrance. It's dark, the majority of hospital staff having gone home hours ago. I switch on the table lamp between two rows of chairs.

"Why are you here?" Brax guides Rhys into a chair before sitting himself.

"Ghost hunting," Lia supplies.

Brax raises his dark brows at me. "Here?" He glances around. "Are there a lot of them?"

"Long story." I grab the tissue box from the front desk and set it on the table near Rhys. "Tell me what happened."

Rhys sags in the chair and Brax's much bigger hand engulfs his, before he explains. "Todd Springer booked a room for the weekend. He and his fiancée, Sandra, wanted to find a quaint, out of the way spot to marry and saw our place on the Chamber's website. Sandra was meeting him here tomorrow."

Their place is next door to my home and business, The

Wedding Chapel. We enjoy being close to each other, and often share clients. "How sad."

Rhys sobs. "What are we going to tell her?"

A male voice intrudes. "I've already contacted Ms. Norwalk." Detective Landon Jones, my sometimes nemesis, strolls up to us. He's in uniform, even though it's after midnight, and the bags under his eyes are larger than usual. His customary notepad is in hand, and he looks to be reviewing something he has written there. "Since Mr. Springer has no living next of kin, she was his emergency contact."

"It was going to be so perfect," Rhys says. I hand him a tissue and he dabs at his eyes. "They were going to fall in love with the B&B, hire Ava to plan the ceremony, Queenie would cater it, and..." He leans forward, covering his face.

Brax pats his back.

Jones glances at them. "I'll need a statement from each of you." He flicks a curious gaze at me and Lia. "What are you doing here, Fantome?"

He wouldn't believe me if I told him. I stop myself from correcting his version of my last name. I'm married now, and I prefer both Fantome and Cross. He knows this and purposely doesn't use the hyphenated name. "Helping Lia with a homework assignment," I say, before she can mention ghosts.

"At this time on a Saturday night?"

Brax clears his throat, taking the spotlight off me. "What can we tell you, detective?"

Jones stares at me a for a tense moment, as if reluctant to let it go, but then turns his attention to Brax. "Was the deceased acting depressed or upset about anything? The upcoming nuptials, possibly?"

My friend shakes his head. "He seemed fine. I mean, he'd only just arrived this evening and he didn't talk much. Quiet sort. Asked to take his dinner in the room, but he didn't seemed depressed."

Rhys waves the tissue. "He said he couldn't wait for Sandra to see the place. Said they had a lot to discuss and the 'calming vibe,'"—he makes air quotes—"would be good for her."

"Why would he jump then?" I ask. "He doesn't sound suicidal."

Jones' lips firm. "Do not stick your nose into this," he warns. "It's clear cut."

Rhys nods. "We found a note."

It's rare I wish for a spirit to speak to me, but this is one of those times. Unfortunately, Mr. Springer is AWOL. Maybe he's crossed over. "Doesn't it seem odd that he would plan this weekend, only to take his own life?"

Jones sighs audibly to let me know he doesn't appreciate my speculation. "Some folks seek out a place away from their home to end things. They don't want to leave their family and friends with the memory of their death in their own home."

It's a good argument, but I'm unconvinced, since our ghost has insisted differently. Getting Jones to believe me will be tricky, however, since he detests my ghost-whispering skills, and I have no proof, outside of a dead man's claims.

"Was the note handwritten?" Lia asks.

We all turn to her. Jones puts his hands on his hips. "Young lady, you should be home in bed. It's past curfew."

"I have a permission slip from my guidance counselor." She opens her backpack and digs around. "I'm staying overnight with Ava. You can call my mom, if you want.

She'll confirm it, but she's asleep by now. You might not want to wake her up. She's really grouchy if she doesn't get her eight hours, you know. Circadian rhythms and all that."

This is news to me. The staying overnight part. Might be a good idea for me to take the girl and vamoose. "Detective Jones is right." The words stick on my tongue, but I sound as polite as ever. I stand and motion her toward the exit. "We should go and let him do his job."

Brax and Rhys come to their feet as well, and we exchange hugs. "What am I going to say to her?" Rhys asks. I assume he's talking about Sandra. "Is there any way you could, you know, do the thing?"

The thing, as in séance? I force myself not to look at Jones. "Let's discuss it later, okay? I'll be over after we have brunch with Mama and Daddy."

We say our goodbyes and Lia and I leave. At the car, she shoves her backpack into the backseat. "What about Avenger? Are we coming back to talk to him?"

I am. "Right now, we're going home. We can't help anyone, ghost or living, if we're exhausted."

"I'm not tired."

That makes one of us. I put the car in gear and drive down the sloping hill of the hospital. Lights are on in a few of the rooms high overhead. "I didn't realize you were spending the night."

"Did I forget to mention that?" When I glance over, her grin is charming. "I told Mom you needed a software upgrade that required I take your site offline for a while. Better to do that at night, you know."

"You lied to your mother. Not cool, Lia."

She fingers one of her curls and the smile disappears. "I

did not. I *am* doing a software upgrade, and I mentioned we were ghost hunting. She's totally cool with it."

What I suspect her mom fails to understand is that ghosts are real. "You told her the *hunt* was at the morgue?"

"Well, duh." Her indignant tone is total bravado. "She likes me hanging out with you."

A sharp pain sets up shop at the base of my skull. "We will tell her that it was at the morgue tomorrow."

"*Avaaa!*" It comes out a whine. "She doesn't care, honestly. I've been in worse places with my friends. I swear."

"We are not lying to your mother."

"I didn't lie! I just didn't tell her exactly where we were searching for a ghost."

Mrs. Chen will probably want to kill both of us. She isn't exactly a helicopter parent from what I've seen, but what mother is okay with her kid hanging out in a bone house? "I'll do what I can to reassure her that your interest in the dead isn't morbid or bad for your health, but..." What am I saying? Of course it's morbid, and it might *actually* be bad for her. I've never raised a child, how would I know? "This is a small town and gossip is rampant. She'll find out, no matter how you try to hide it, and then we'll both be in worse shape. Plus, I don't keep secrets."

"You want to ruin my life, don't you?"

The pain sharpens. "Your life is not ruined if we're honest with her. Just let me handle it, all right? I promise I'll make sure you get to continue working with me."

"And hunting ghosts?"

Lord, help me. "Only if you agree to be totally forthcoming with me and her from now on."

She slumps in the seat. "Fine."

Wiggling a finger at her, I don't let her off the hook. "Come on, let me hear it. Give me your word."

"Word."

This girl. "*Lia.*"

"I promise to tell you and my mother the truth from here on out."

"And not leave out pertinent details."

Her sigh is Oscar-worthy. "You're a hardas—"

"Lia!"

"Ugh!" She shakes her fist at the roof. "I will tell you all the *pertinent* details. Mom, too. I swear. Want me to open a vein and seal the deal with my blood?"

"Yes," I reply sarcastically, "and sacrifice a goat at the full moon. Deal?"

Her demeanor shifts so fast it gives me whiplash. She laughs, the sound echoing in the car. "You're hysterical." She toys with her spirit box. "Now, what are we doing about the B&B ghost?"

THREE

When we arrive at The Wedding Chapel, the lights are on upstairs. I park and we get out, and I see Logan next door at the B&B with Queenie, Brax's mother, on the front porch.

She paces under the lights, her long skirt whipping back and forth, while a couple loads their luggage into the trunk of a big Lincoln. Her kinky black hair is loose, an unusual sight, and waving around like her skirts. She's formidable, and a successful businesswoman in her own right, but at that moment, she's just a mother fighting for her child. "Please, won't you stay?" Queenie begs.

Crickets and other night insects are silent, the stars hiding behind gray clouds, as I haul out my bag. I imagine Queenie was sleeping when Brax called her to come over. Logan lifts his chin in greeting to me, remaining quiet as the male guest looks back at her.

"We wanted a quiet weekend, not"—he waves a hand at nothing in particular—"this."

He's short and balding. His wife, who's taller and a bit

thin, throws her purse into the front seat. "I'm so sorry," she says in a soft, Southern accent. "We really aren't comfortable staying here now."

Logan's calm voice floats across the lawn as he attempts to quell Queenie's anxiety. His tousled hair the color of toasted pecans, classic nose, and tanned skin. Easygoing with a casual sexiness that I adore. "This will all look different in the morning," he tells the pair. "You've had a terrible upset, but if you would wait until then, I'm sure you'll see that this is the perfect vacation spot for you."

Lia and I hustle up the concrete drive. "Tough to find a place to stay at this time of the night—uh, morning," I correct, purposely glancing at my watch. "I don't know anyone around here who'll take folks so late. The Nottingham is the closest hotel, a good twenty minutes from here, and..." I lower my voice dramatically. "I hear it's haunted."

They stare at each other over the hood. "We'll drive to Atlanta," the man says, more to his wife than to us. "Then on home tomorrow."

"You should be in the city around sunrise." I join Logan and Queenie. Across the street, I see Sage still has her lights on at the teahouse. I'm slightly surprised she isn't over here investigating. "Check-in at most places isn't until three p.m., so you'll have some time to kill." To Brax's mother, I murmur, "Get me one of the discount cards and a pen."

Logan sidles up to me as she hurries inside. "Strong arguments," he murmurs in my ear. "You'd make a good trial lawyer."

Hardly. "That's your domain. I'm better at business transactions."

Lia sits in a rocking chair. Logan motions at her. "I see a stray followed you home."

She sticks her tongue out. "Hey, I'm her sidekick. A good one, I'll have you know."

Queenie rushes back out, handing me the items I've requested. I scribble on it and march down the steps. "Whether you want to leave a nice, comfortable bed here and drive through the night to Atlanta, or stay until morning, where you'll enjoy a hot breakfast made by the best cook in these parts"—I point at Queenie, who is chewing her thumbnail—"or not, here is a fifty percent discount for one night, and I'm throwing in a bonus on any of my event planning packages. If you have a birthday, family reunion, or even a girls' night out coming up, let me know and I'll handle all the details."

The woman accepts the card. "Why, my grandmother is celebrating her seventieth in November." She glances at her husband. "We certainly could use help with that."

"Wonderful. If you stay, we can pull together some ideas tomorrow."

Everyone seems to hold their breath as a silent communication takes place between the couple. I know the looks they are exchanging and step back, giving them space.

"When my grandfather turned seventy," Lia calls to the woman, "I made this cool book for him—Seventy Things I Love About You. He went nuts for it. I gathered pictures from his different decades and added them, plus photos of him and mom, him and me. He carried it everywhere until he passed. I have it now, and I go through it all the time."

The woman faces her and smiles. "What a wonderful idea." She grabs her purse and slides the card into it. "Hon? What do you think?"

Her husband makes a grumbling noise, unconvinced but seemingly less adamant about their exit.

It's important to know when to push, as well as when to back off. "Well," I say, "it was nice meeting y'all. We'll let you be. Have a good drive, and let us know you made it to Atlanta safe."

I wave and motion the others to the entrance.

"You are a sly one, Ava Fantome-Cross," Logan says in my ear.

The couple are engaging in a heated whisper-fest and I hope they do indeed stay. With the heatwave, our tourism has declined in recent weeks, and the B&B has had too many vacancies.

Inside, Queenie continues to pace and wring her hands. "That poor man. And my boys!" Her layers of beaded bracelets jingle as she rubs her eyes. "This type of publicity could ruin them."

It's typical in the South to focus on the worst possible outcome. I rub her shoulders. "They're not ruined. Whatever comes of this, Brax is a wonderful marketer. He'll turn any negative publicity around and make gold from it."

She clasps my hands like I'm a lifeline. "How can you know?"

I wink. "Because he takes after his mother."

This brings a smile to her face and she releases her grip. "You're always so confident, Ava."

Hardly. I do know how to put on a good front, though. I am my mother's daughter. "Anything bad comes of this, I'll put Dixie on it."

Queenie laughs. "She hears you callin' her by her given name, she'll tan your hide."

My mother has never raised a hand to me and we both know she never would. Her best friend is simply stressed.

Some of that disappears when the couple open the front door and stick their heads in. "We'll stay," the husband says, and adds, "for now."

His wife holds up the card. "I'll take you up on this offer."

Queenie claps and motions them in the rest of the way. "Let's get you back upstairs. Would you like a nightcap?"

He sets down the suitcases. "Do you have anything stronger than wine?"

With a conspiratory wink, she leans toward him. "I know where the good stuff is hidden. Follow me."

"We can talk in the morning," I tell his wife. She nods and trails after Queenie and her husband.

Logan puts an arm around my shoulders and guides me out and over to The Wedding Chapel. Lia follows.

My grandmother, in her cat form, eyes us as we come up the steps. She's a witch who's managed to extend her life by shapeshifting into a feline. Her tail moves lazily through the air and she narrows her eyes at us from her perch in a rocking chair. The gargoyles at the top of the stair railings talk to each other. "There's a bad wind blowing," one says.

"Evil is brewing," the other adds.

Yes, my grandmother is a shape-shifting cat and I can hear inanimate objects. I don't have the energy for their nonsense and ignore all of them.

Inside, Logan asks about our experience at the morgue. Lia and I describe it briefly over cups of herbal tea Sage gave me for my occasional insomnia. Before I'm halfway through my portion, my lids are drooping.

"I have doubts about the man taking his own life," I tell

Logan, "but his ghost was like many who are freshly deceased—erratic and unreliable. He could be confused."

"Persephone's not around?" Logan asks.

"Haven't heard hide nor hair of her." My spirit guide, who claims she's a guardian angel, is often as unreliable as the specters. "And now I have a client to appease tomorrow on my day off." It's worth it, though, if it helps Brax and Rhys. "I better get some sleep."

Lia tells me she'll wash up the cups and I barely make it upstairs to bed before I'm comatose. I've had enough of the dead *and* the living for one day, and I'm thankful when Logan tucks me in and I can forget about ghosts for a while.

FOUR

Sunday, I cancel brunch with Mama and Daddy, but they understand, considering what has occurred.

Since I sleep late, I end up eating breakfast at lunch, and discover Sage has wandered over to help Lia prepare eggs, biscuits, and fried potatoes. The four of us dig in and don't come up for air until the food is gone.

"So what's the deal with the dead guy?" Sage asks, refilling coffee cups. She's a natural born witch and a good friend, helping deal with uncooperative spirits and cursed objects. Today, she's in yoga pants and a long tunic with the words "Go fly" on it and a graphic of a broom.

"Supposedly jumped out the window," I tell her. She recently had Queenie give her corn rows and has them piled on top of her hair in a messy bun that looks totally natural but would take me hours to recreate. "But his ghost claimed he would never take his own life. Could be an accident."

"I thought he left a note indicating it was intentional," Logan says, after thanking Sage for the refill.

I finish the last biscuit, which I've covered in Mama's

homemade blackberry jam. "Doesn't fit with an accident, I guess. Maybe he's simply confused."

"Notes can be forged," Lia states. "Maybe he was pushed."

Sage sets the carafe on the counter and returns to her seat across from me. "By someone at the B&B?"

"Seems highly unlikely. The only other folks there at the time were the couple we met, and Brax and Rhys."

"Either way, this is Detective Jones' territory." Logan says. His tone has the ring of a warning.

"Amen." I chug my coffee and nod so he won't worry. "Lia, we need to get you home and talk to your mother."

"Already? Can't I stay a little longer?"

"You can come help me at the shop." Sage folds her napkin in half and grabs her messenger bag from the back of the chair. "I have Helen's tea party this afternoon and Raven can't help with her ankle."

A few weeks ago, her sister, Raven, fell from a ladder at the Chicks With Gifts Emporium that they own, and broke it. According to Sage, she's a bear about it, too, hating the fact she can't get around like normal and had to hire extra help.

Lia's eyes brighten. "Can I?" she pleads to me.

"You can ask your mom when we see her."

She tosses her napkin at me. "You're such a downer."

"You're lucky you aren't my daughter or you'd see what a true downer I can be."

Tabby meows from her spot in a shaft of sunlight on the floor, as if she agrees I'm less than a fun person. I stick my tongue out at her.

Rising, I stack the dirty plates. "Before anyone goes, however, there is something I want to say." I look each of them in the eyes. "If you ever feel as if you don't matter, or this world is too much for you, I want you to talk to me. I can't promise not to try and change your mind about suicide, but I can give you some intel on what it's like on the other side. You all are loved and you matter very much to me."

Sage rolls her eyes but smiles. Lia jumps up and pounces on me, wrapping her arms around my middle. Logan reaches over and squeezes my hand.

An hour later, I'm seated in a tiny kitchen nook across from Lia's mom. A tiny woman with coal black hair, bangs, and thick glasses, Mrs. Chen smiles, her sunny disposition making it hard not to feel like life is good and nothing can disturb her inner calm. I pray that's true. "Lia wasn't entirely forthcoming with you about her visit last night."

The girl in question disappeared to her room as soon she'd greeted her mom.

Mrs. Chen chuckles. "Doesn't surprise me. She's a handful."

That's an understatement. "She did perform the software upgrade for me." At least she claims to have finished it while I was asleep. I wouldn't know the difference either way. There's no good way to explain the next part so I spit it out. "But we spent several hours at the hospital morgue last night trying to chat with a ghost who is giving the place trouble."

Her eyes crinkle at the corners as her smile grows. "I bet she loved that."

Hmm. "You're okay with it?"

"Of course."

Lia barrels into the kitchen holding up her phone. "You'll never guess who texted me!"

We both stare at her.

"Carlyn! She invited me to her house tonight to binge

the Marvel movies!" She squeals and twirls on sock-clad feet, holding the phone to her heart. "What if she likes me, Mom?"

Mrs. Chen takes her hand. "Why wouldn't she? You're odd, but special."

Lia squeals again and races out. "I've got to figure out what to wear."

Mrs. Chen, and her smile, refocus on me. "Whatever makes my daughter happy, makes me happy. She is...unique. You see?"

"I do," I reassure her. Nothing like your mother telling you you're *odd, but special.* I almost chuckle, thinking that's one Mama might have used on me when I was Lia's age. "She's welcome at my house anytime, and I'll do my best to watch out for her."

"You don't mind that she's...?"

"Obsessed with ghosts?"

The smile falters. "That she likes girls as well as boys."

Ah. "Makes no difference to me." I rise from the chair, checking the time. Logan is waiting to take me to the hospital to see if I can raise either Avenger or Mr. Springer. "Earlier, she expressed interest in helping my friend with a party at the new tea shop. Do you think that's still a possibility or should I let Sage know she won't be able to now that she has a date?"

"I'm here." Lia appears in the doorway, out of breath. "I need to go, Mom. I need to work. Otherwise, I'll fixate on my hair and I'll... I'll..."

"Go." Her mother makes cheerful shooing motions. "Don't drop any of those fancy tea cups, you hear?"

Lia hugs her and we're out the door. My phone buzzes

with a text as we're heading for the car. Logan is leaning on the hood as I check the screen.

It's from Sage. SOS. *911! Need help!*

I frown. Logan boosts off the car. "What is it?"

I dial Sage's number, but it goes to voicemail. "Not sure." I show him the text. "She's not answering."

"My mother is probably giving her grief about something." He holds the door for me and then climbs in on the driver's side. "Should we head there instead of the hospital?"

"Lia's cleared to help at the party, so we should drop her off first." I try calling Sage again. Still no answer. My worry meter heads for the red zone. "I hope nothing is seriously wrong."

"She's a witch, isn't she?" Lia asks from the backseat. "Can't she handle just about anything with a spell or a potion or something?"

Sage has handled a lot in the short time I've known her. Logan is probably right—it's his mother getting under her skin. "I'm sure she's fine, but let's find out."

FIVE

Food may be the Southern equivalent of love, but tea is a close second. As we arrive at Tea Leaves, I'm worried about my friend, but also thinking I need to buy a pound of her lemon raspberry blend. I'm obsessed with it.

While there's a car parked in front of the B&B, the parking lot of the tea shop is empty. The front door is locked and Logan peers in a window. "Uh oh."

Lia and I rush to his side. Through the lace curtains, I notice the usual café tables have been pushed out of the center of the showroom to make room for a long, rectangular one. A decorative pink and white cloth covers the top, and eight chairs are gathered around it.

On top of the glass display case nearby sit vintage china plates and cups in stacks, none of them matching but Sage's eye for color and design created a lovely cohesiveness. Tiers of confections, trays of her signature fudge, and several wooden boxes containing a variety of teas wait for the party to begin. Fairy lights twine around the center candelabra and wink at us.

"What is it?" Lia turns her head this way and that to peer through the holes in the lace. "Where is she?"

Logan tries the door again. "You don't see it?"

My gaze lands on something slithering around the candelabra. "Holy smokes," I say, taking a step back. "Is that what I think it is?"

Reaching into his pocket, he fumbles for his keys. He owns the building and rents it to her. "I hope she had the good sense to get out of there."

Lia still has her face pressed against the window. "What are you guys talking about? I don't see anything. Is it a ghost?"

"No," I say as Logan finds the right key and sticks it in the lock. "In the center of the table." I point.

She squints, and then the thing moves. She jumps a foot, knocking into me. "Twisting serpent," she whispers. "What is *that* doing in there?"

It isn't just any snake—it's a copperhead, one of the most poisonous around these parts, and a good four feet long. Logan throws open the door, and glances at the two of us. "Stay here. I'll take care of it."

I motion him forward. "Don't be ridiculous. I'm helping."

"I'll stay here," Lia calls as we hurry inside.

Skirting past the table, I dash for the rear. "Sage! Are you okay?"

"Ava?" Her voice is weak. I discover her standing on her work counter in back, wringing her hands. Her phone lays on the floor a few feet away. "Thank the goddess you're here."

Logan joins us, scanning the room. "Is there more than one?"

She shakes her head. "I don't think so." She spins in a circle. "Do you think there is? Do they hang out in pairs or something?"

Since I've never seen her scared in the time I've know her, not even when facing down ghosts, her current bearing surprises me. "Not that I know of." I reach out to offer her a hand and help her down. "Logan will take care of it. You're safe."

"I need a broom and a towel," he says. "Preferably a big one that's thick and heavy."

She motions at a stack of folded bar towels on a shelf. "That's all I've got."

He frowns. "Where's your broom?"

"You think because I'm a witch, I naturally have one hanging around?"

"I think because you own a store that needs a good sweep at times, you might."

"We don't live in the Stone Age. I have a robot vacuum." She points toward the corner where a squat black disc sits on the floor.

"Too bad that couldn't suck up a snake." Lia laughs.

We all glance at the opening where she now stands. She hitches a thumb over her shoulder. "Folks are arriving for the party. I closed and locked the door."

"I'm cursed," Sage says.

"No, you're not." I light a flame under the kettle on her stove. "When you run a business, things happen. You've got this."

Logan takes the stairs that lead to the second-floor apartment two at a time. I assume he is going for a towel that might actually cover the intruder.

Lia picks up the phone and hands it to Sage. "Can't you put a spell on it or something?"

"I can't even stand to look at it." The witch shivers visibly. "In general, I don't care much about snakes, but copperheads freak me out."

"As they do most of us." I consider our options. "Do you want me to send Helen and the others away?"

"It's my first big party." Sage appears on the verge of crying. "If I cancel last minute, she'll ruin me."

Logan's mother is a force of nature in Thornhollow. While the slithering visitor is unexpected, if word got out one had been inside, I'd be Sage's only customer from here on out.

Logan bounds into the room and jets past us. He carries a thick bath towel and a large brown jute bag that once held coffee beans. "Got it covered. Ava, distract my mother. Sage, get down from there and be prepared to let me out the back exit. Lia, as soon as the snake and I are gone, you set that table."

"I love it when you take charge." I follow him to the front, considering different ideas to stall his mother and the other guests.

Sage peeks through the opening, waves her hand at the table, and mutters under her breath. "That will keep them from seeing you," she says to Logan.

I grab a tray of fudge and a stack of pretty pink napkins, giving the table a wide berth. Glancing back, I watch my husband ambush the snake from behind, tossing the towel over it. It wriggles frantically and my breath catches. "Be careful," I say quietly but with urgency.

Logan winks. "Don't worry. I know what I'm doing."

Maybe he does. He's told me plenty of stories about him and his brother, Charlie, spending their youth at their family's winery chasing off everything from mice and snakes to raccoons and opossums to keep them from the grapevines and their fruit. He also went to summer camp at the nearby lake for many years. While he considered communing with the outdoors great fun, some of his stories about the crazy things the campers did to each other, including putting harmless snakes in each other's beds, have given me nightmares.

The snake continues to whip back and forth, drawing closer to the edge of the table but still blinded, thanks to the towel. Logan grabs the candelabra and uses it to slide the slippery thing the rest of the way off. It falls into the open jute bag.

He closes the end and starts for the rear. Blowing out a relieved breath, I take the tray and head out the front.

"Lovely day, isn't it?" Holding the fudge in front of me, I create a barrier and close the door.

This causes both Helen and the woman next to her to step back. She's dressed as if she's come straight from church, even though it's mid-afternoon. It's ninety and humid, yet she's model perfect.

"Avalon." My mother-in-law offers me a tight smile, her tone suggesting she is less than happy to see me. "What a lovely surprise."

Liar. "Fudge?"

"We're here for a party." She glances over as two more of her friends join us. "We really should get inside."

She reaches for the knob and I block it with my hip. "Sage is putting the finishing touches on a few things. She asked me to bring you these. Here,"—I hold out the tray to those gathering. What woman isn't distracted by homemade chocolate?—"try one. They're absolutely to die for. She makes each batch herself."

Three of the women's eyes light up and they select a piece. The woman next to Helen, whose name I can't remember, eyes me with suspicion from under her ridiculously flamboyant mint green hat. "Do you work here, too? I thought your mama said you were having success with Wilhelmina's business."

More than I could dream of. "Just helping my friend. Sage has done such a great job with the place, and I know you'll have fun today."

"If we ever get in," Helen mumbles, giving me a pointed look.

I shove the tray in front of her face once more. "Really, you have to try one." Hopefully, it will make her shut up. "Sage wants everything to be perfect before you come in."

"I don't believe we saw you in church this morning," her friend says.

"Late night." I recognize her now. "It's Mrs. Danube, correct? I'd shake your hand but..." I give a hapless shrug.

Logan appears from around the side of the house, smiling wide. No sign of the bag or any snake in sight. "Mother." He joins us on the porch and kisses her cheek, then nods at the other women. "Ladies."

Already blissed out from chocolate, they grin and titter at his handsome face. Pink napkins flutter everywhere. He has that effect on most women.

"I'm so glad you're here," he says. "Sage has talked nonstop about this since you booked it. She's so excited to have you be her first official guests."

My tray is nearly empty, except for two remaining pieces and a few napkins. I lean my head lightly against Logan's shoulder. "You're going to have her read your tea leaves, right? She's so accurate."

"So we've heard." Helen seems to catch on that we're buying Sage more time. "Shall we try this chocolate, Maxine?"

Mrs. Danube reluctantly fingers the last piece as Helen daintily takes a bite of hers. As they chew, they both seem genuinely impressed. I would talk about the ingredients, or her process, except I know nothing about either so I smile and nod, and rack my brain for a new distraction.

Logan sneaks his arm around me and squeezes my shoulder gently. I sense that he, too, is struggling to figure out what to do next.

"Well," Helen says. "Now, I definitely need some tea. How much longer do you think Sage will be?"

Logan and I exchange a glance. Before either of us can respond, the door behind us opens.

We whirl to find Lia, an apron embroidered with *Tea Leaves* and a tea cup under the words, is over her clothes. She tilts her nose up and motions the group inside. "Welcome to Tea Leaves Emporium. Won't you come in?"

SIX

Sage begs me to stay, and I do, but I keep out of sight as much as possible in the backroom. I keep busy heating water for more tea and refilling trays of desserts.

Once the group is mostly done with their refreshments, the real action begins. I listen as Sage talks them through the divinations revealed at the bottom of their cups.

"I see an acorn," she tells one of the women. "Improved health and possibly an unexpected windfall is coming your way."

Another has a star. "This predicts great happiness."

Helen's reveals a boat. "A friend is coming for a visit." She also has a basket. "And this denotes an addition to your family, by marriage, birth, or adoption."

"Hmm," I hear Helen say, "perhaps there's a grandchild on the way."

Lia, eavesdropping with me, elbows my side and snorts.

I smile but shake my head, hoping it's not Trysta who might be pregnant. I've enjoyed a cup of my favorite blend and study the leftover leaves to see if I have the gift of tasseomancy. All I see is a wet blob.

After the readings are over, she and I are removing plates and bagging up purchases from the tiny selection of items Sage has for sale, when I notice a car pull in front of the B&B. The woman driving it is dressed in gray from head to toe, including three-inch heels, and looks to have been crying. Sandra Norwalk, the deceased's fiancée, no doubt.

Things go without a hitch until Lia comes from the storage area, where I've sent her to retrieve a stack of cardboard drink carriers. She has an odd look on her face.

"Are you okay?" I ask.

She's pale and has forgotten the carrier trays. "I don't think so."

"Was it the snake?" Logan had assured me before he left that the copperhead was going to find a much better home. "I thought it was gone."

"Do you think Sage *is* cursed?"

I grab the girl's shoulders. "Of course not. What's the matter?"

"Could I be cursed? Like, is it contagious?"

"Lia, where is this coming from?"

Sage appears, carrying an empty tray. Her face is flushed and she's smiling. "Time to read the leaves." The way she says it, this sounds like the best day ever. "Do you want to stick around and hear what they have to say?"

"Sure," Lia says, but she sounds less than excited. "I'll be there in a minute."

When Sage exits, Lia gets a drink of water, still looking frazzled. "You know that game in the storeroom? The one with the creepy guy behind the glass?"

"The fortune teller machine?" Sage bought it from an

antiques dealer in Story Cove. The Zultan mannequin sits in the top half with a crystal ball, with a sultan-like mustache and beard, and a bejeweled scarf wrapped around his head. You put in a quarter and he spits out a prediction about your future. I think he's creepy. "She's going to clean it up, get it working again, and put it out on the floor to add atmosphere. Why?"

Lia holds out a piece of card stock with scrolls and words on it. "It works."

"What? It's not even plugged in, is it?"

She juts her chin at the card. "I don't think it needs to be."

I snag the message from her grasp. *Danger from the beyond awaits.*

No wonder she looks like someone has kicked her. "It's just a dumb old machine, a carnival trick. It doesn't mean anything."

"I wanna go home now," she says.

"Lia, seriously, it's for entertainment. Granted, it's sick entertainment, but..."

She nods. "Yeah, I get it. I know it's not real."

I can't convince her to stay. While I want to listen in on the readings, especially my mother-in-law's, and help Sage clean up, I remove my apron. "I'll take you. You have to get ready for that movie marathon tonight." I hope that mentioning this might lift her spirits.

"Right."

Oh boy. Not even that brings a smile to her face. I want to kick that machine.

We're heading out when the woman from the B&B comes running across the street waving at me. "There you are. I wanted to speak to you about the birthday celebration."

My weekends are rarely relaxing but this one hadn't even provided a few hours rest. "Yes, of course. I need to run my friend home first. Give me twenty minutes and we can discuss it."

"Oh, I thought we might have some tea." She points at the shop.

"I would love that as soon as I return."

Persephone appears right behind the woman, hovering a few inches off the ground. She's been MIA for weeks, and I have to admit it's been both nice and a bit worrisome. "Have Logan take Lia home."

Of course, neither my protégé, nor the new client, can see or hear her. She certainly helps me through some tricky situations, but sometimes her input and assistance are taxing to say the least. She can't come right out and tell me things, only coach me to figure them out on my own. Drives me batty.

From the probing stare she bestows on the woman, I figure there's something I need to learn about Todd Springer's death, and the gal might be able to tell me what it is.

As if Persephone has summoned him, Logan appears on the porch of The Wedding Chapel. "How's it going?" he calls to me. He's probably been watching the place with an eagle eye, praying his mother behaves and there are no more snakes.

I paste on a smile and wave. "Could you take Lia home for me?"

He nods. "Sure thing."

Leaving her in his care, I extend a hand. "Ava Fantome-Cross. Nice to formally meet you."

"Jill Carr." We shake. "I looked you up online. You get lots of nice reviews."

I hate to intrude on the private party, so I motion her to an outside table on the veranda. "I'll get us some tea in a moment. You mentioned a birthday celebration for your grandmother. Seventy, right? That's a big one."

"We wanted to take her on a cruise, but she's having issues with her joints. Plus, she's legally blind. She doesn't like traveling far from home. I still want to throw her a party and I need a nice venue that's handicap accessible. Many of her friends are up there in years, too, and have trouble with stairs."

Persephone levitates in the yard between us and the sidewalk. Her attention is on the B&B.

"Have you considered booking the Cross Winery? They have a fantastic setup for large crowds, and have hosted dozens of parties. Totally accessible. I can get you a discount." I wink. "I'm in good with the owners."

"The vineyard? I thought I recognized that name. It could work, I suppose."

"November is a pretty time. Mrs. Cross will have it decorated for the holidays."

Her face lights up. "Oh, that would be fun."

As I list ideas for her to consider, Todd's fiancée makes an appearance, Rhys right behind her as she crosses the porch and heads down the steps, wobbling a bit on her heels. She's wiping her cheeks with a tissue and he's sympathizing. Brax follows, carrying a soft-sided suitcase.

Jill shifts in her seat, glancing at them. "Sad, isn't it? I can't imagine how I'd be if Gordon did such a thing."

"I feel bad for all involved," I say. Persephone turns to me and motions to keep talking. I grasp at something to ask.

"Did you meet Mr. Springer? Was he acting odd in any way?"

Clearly uncomfortable, she shakes her head dismissively, and turns to look through the curtained window when the women inside laugh uproariously. "The detective asked me the same thing. Our paths never crossed."

Brax situates the suitcase in Sandra's car; she hugs Rhys, her sobs echoing over to us. Knowing him and his soft heart, he's crying, too.

"It seems strange," I continue, Persephone glaring at me and making that stupid *go on* motion with her hand again. "From what Brax and Rhys told me, he seemed happy enough. I know people with depression often wear a mask and can appear that way, but it's tragic since he had a lot to live for with his upcoming wedding and all."

She's silent and a glance at her shows her lips have firmed and she is worrying her necklace. Her cheeks have flushed in the heat. "He left a note, right? It claimed he 'couldn't do this anymore.'"

"Is that what it said?" Had she seen the note? "Are you the one who found him?"

"Heavens, no!" She gives an incredulous laugh. "I was nowhere near him. It was late and Gordon said he couldn't sleep, so he went downstairs to the library to find something to read. I drew a bath—I brought these new tropical salts with me, and I was thankful for time alone, if you know what I mean. We've been so busy and stressed out lately, I needed this weekend away."

"I'm sorry it's turned out not to be very relaxing."

She waves it off like a pesky fly. "My lot in life, believe me. Anyway..." She peers in the window again. "Can I get some iced tea? It's quite hot out here."

"Yes, of course. In fact, Mrs. Cross is at the party. I don't want to crash it, but perhaps when it's over, I can pull her aside and the three of us can discuss your grandmother's birthday."

"I'd like that."

Our timing is good, since the group is breaking up. Sage wears a smile, but I can see the strain behind her eyes. I introduce Jill to Helen and offer to help Sage clean. She gets Jill an iced raspberry tea and practically drags me to the back.

"What's wrong?" I ask quietly.

Her face is ashen. "This."

She holds out a cup with wet tea leaves in the bottom. I know I'm supposed to be shocked or worried, but I have no idea what message they're conveying. They simply look like a blob of soot. "And you interpreted this to mean what?"

A frustrated breath blows out her lips and she points at the divinatory leaves. "Don't you see it?"

I shake my head. "Sorry, no."

She twists the cup to a new angle. "Now?"

"There's a blotch there, a smear, and a smaller glob up here." Minus cat hair, it's not all that dissimilar to the stomach contents Tabby occasionally leaves in my shoes. "Is it a fat version of the Space Needle?"

The crease between her dark brows deepens and she snatches it from my hands. "How can you joke about this?"

"I don't even know what *this* is!"

At my raised tone, she glances over her shoulder.

"Everything all right back there?" Helen calls.

"Fine," Sage replies and lowers her voice once more. "It's the grim, Ava."

"What?" I grab the cup and look at it again. Still looks

like nothing to me. "How do you get a grim reaper out of that?"

"Not a reaper, the hound."

A dog? "You mean like in Harry Potter?"

Restraining her impatience makes her nearly vibrate. "Yes, like that."

"Doesn't that portent turn out to be a nice shifter guy?"

She tosses her hands up and turns. "Goddess be, you are impossible."

"You're not alone in that belief. Mama has said it a million times."

My humor is lost on her.

"I'm serious. First the message from Zultan, then the snake, now this."

"You got a message from the carnival game?"

Her eyes are frightened. "He said, 'the reaper is coming.' Then I get the grim in my tea leaves."

She's terribly upset, and I feel my own calm starting to fade. What did the gargoyles say last night?

There's a bad wind blowing,

Evil is brewing.

Shaking it off, I place the cup in the sink and pat her shoulder. "You've had a rough day. Why don't you head home and I'll finish here?"

Fingering her apron, she shakes her head. "I can handle it. You have a client. Go..."—she shoos me off—"do whatever you do with them."

First Lia, now Sage. I'm batting zero for two so far, and what's up with that stupid Zultan?

Mentally, I call for Persephone. Maybe she can help. "I'll be back in a minute," I tell Sage, and head to the front.

Jill is going out the door, the bell tinkling at her exit, her cell to her ear. Helen is writing something on the back of one of Sage's business cards. She hands it to me. "The date is set and she would like a tea party theme." She whirls her pen around at the room. "She likes this decor, for whatever reason. She's planning for a hundred guests, and I quoted her seventeen dollars a plate for finger foods. She negotiated down to fifteen, and she'll provide the cake. Here's her email so you can send her the contract."

"Wow, okay." I accept the card. "Do I owe you a fee?"

Her smile is cunning. "It's not the first time I've done your job for you, so maybe I should start charging you."

She's sent a good deal of business my way, but I'd hardly say she's done my job for me. Still, I work hard to stay on her good side for Logan's sake. I give her a gracious nod. "And I appreciate it."

"We have details to work out about your wedding and reception in October. Dinner Wednesday night. Leave that cat at home."

I track where her pen points and see Tabby cleaning herself on a chair at the end of the table. "Tabitha," I chastise, using her full name to get my grandmother's attention, "you can't be in here."

She jumps down and darts for the back. Sage emerges at that moment to begin picking up the plates and tea cups.

"Oh, Sage." Helen stops and pockets her pen. "Today was lovely, but I have a few suggestions. I'll email you my list tomorrow."

She exits and Sage pauses. "I'm not intimidated by anyone, but that woman scares me."

"Welcome to my world."

Through the window, I notice Detective Jones has pulled in across the street and has the grieving fiancée on the porch, notebook in hand. I'd thought she'd left, but apparently he'd caught her before she could.

Along the side of the house, pretending to be enthralled with the blooming rose bushes, Jill is eavesdropping.

I pocket the business card, and notice the spectral form of a ghost hovering near Sandra and Jones. Todd?

Persephone appears. "Cat first, then ghost."

She vanishes.

"Helpful," I call. "*Not.*"

I discover Tabby in the store room, staring up at the famed Zultan. I swear they're having some kind of mental conversation.

I flip on the overhead light, noticing that shadows still cover the machine, only the painted face spotlighted.

"Sorry to interrupt," I say flippantly. Scooping her up, I scoot back toward the door, the gaze of the carnival fortune teller eerily human. Tabby hisses at me and scrambles in my arms. "Stop it. You don't belong in here."

The machine makes a whirring sound. The head turns and the eyes shift from side to side. "Ava," a man's accented voice says. "Come let Zultan tell your fortune."

I freeze. *That's not creepy at all.* Tabby manages to scratch me and I yelp, dropping her. I tell myself not to engage, but the urge to is overwhelming. "How do you know my name?"

His head tilts and the roaming eyes stop on me. "Zultan knows all."

"Sure you do."

More whirring and a square card pops out of the slot. Against my better judgment, I step forward and swipe it.

SEVEN

"**O**kay, enough." I refuse to be scared of this thing. Or intimidated. I rip up the card with the message, *You will encounter a strange darkness soon,* and toss the pieces in a nearby waste bin. Then I grab a flashlight near the back and return to examine the unit.

"Are you a ghost? Cursed object? Sorry, but you don't scare me. I've dealt with far worse. If you're trapped inside this machine, give me a sign, and I'll get you out."

Sage appears in the doorway. "Are you talking to Zultan?"

Using the beam, I point to the mannequin. "He started it."

She takes the flashlight from my hand, grabs my arm and hauls me out of the room.

"What are you doing?"

"After I get the place tidied up, I'll do a cleansing on the whole building." Persephone hovers near a baking rack, and Sage points to her. "You have something else to take care of."

My spirit guide glares down her nose at me. Apparently

she made sure Sage saw her. "Remember, the ghost across the street?"

I sigh. "Are you sure you're okay?" I ask Sage.

"Of course. It's not the first time I've been cursed."

I struggle not to roll my eyes. Arguing, however, seems futile. "I'll be back later to help."

As I cross the street, Persephone beside me, I send a text to Bis, Sage's boyfriend. I copy it and send the same to Raven. Jill hovers at the rosebushes, taking pictures with her phone out of sight of the detective and Sandra.

Todd's fiancée's face is blotchy, eyes red. She's twisted her handkerchief into a wet mess. Jones sees me and shakes his head, warning me off. The ghost, looking as distraught as Sandra, sees me peering at him and straightens.

"You," he states.

I climb the steps. "Hi, I'm Ava." I say to Sandra, but also for the sake of the earthbound spirit. "I'm so sorry for your loss."

She nods, frowning at my intrusion, but accepting my outstretched hand. "Thank you."

Jones glowers. "We're busy, Ms. Fantome."

"Tell them I didn't jump," Todd urges.

"Fantome-*Cross*, remember?" I smile sweetly at the detective. "I actually came over to speak to Mrs. Carr. I'm helping her arrange a birthday party for her grandmother." I turn toward the rose garden and call, "Jill?"

There's no answer, but Jones comes to his feet, hefting up his pants by his belt. He screws up his lips, understanding why I've interrupted him and Sandra. Together, we venture to the end of the veranda and peer over at where Jill was moments before.

"What are you doing?" Jones asks under his breath.

"She was eavesdropping on your conversation," I tell him. "Thought you might want to conduct your interview in private."

He huffs.

"Is everything okay?" Sandra calls.

"Fine." I absentmindedly wave at her. "Todd's ghost is here," I murmur to Jones, then realize the specter is gone again. "*Was* here. He claims he didn't jump."

Another huff, this one bordering on a growl of frustration. "Can't keep your nose out of my business, can you?"

"You serve and protect the living. I do the same for the dead." I decide to track down Jill. "I'm not sure why she wanted to listen in," I tell him, "but I'll find out. Meanwhile, I suggest you dig deeper into this."

He stands taller, and his accent deepens. "And I suggest y'all go on home before I arrest you for interfering with a police investigation."

I have just stood up to a haunted mannequin. His intimidating tone and glare mean nothing. "So you *are* investigating his death?"

"Go home, Fantome."

"Fantome-Cross. I'm not going home, Detective Jones. I have a ghost to help."

I march down the steps and head around the side of the house. Tabby waits for me, then leads me to the rear lawn. Brax is cleaning the grill. He dwarfs it, even though its ridiculously large and has more buttons and cooking surfaces than my kitchen stove. "Hey." He looks as worn out as I feel. "Get any sleep?"

"Not much. You?"

He puts down his scrub brush and removes his gloves. "None. Jones still out front with Ms. Norwalk?"

I nod. "Did you see Jill come this way?"

He points to the house, his eyes snagging on a section of ground where the spray-painted outline of a body is in stark contrast to the green lawn. The awkward angles of the arms and legs make my stomach tighten. Piano music drifts from the back door. "That's her."

No one has touched the black Baldwin spinet in the parlor in eons. The former owner couldn't even do Chopsticks, but thought the instrument added ambience. "She plays?"

He nods, and wipes the rear of his neck with a handkerchief. "Says it reduces anxiety. She seems to have plenty of that, and isn't sleeping well in my fair establishment. Can't imagine why," he adds with sarcasm.

Glancing up, I study the window Todd fell from. "I have a question about the party she's hired me for."

The music stops abruptly, and a single flat note rings out over and over as if Jill is pounding on the key.

Brax tilts his head toward the house. "We never tuned the thing."

She's obviously embarrassed I caught her snooping, and from the sounds of it, the piano is causing her more anxiety. Forcing a conversation right now could backfire. "Probably better if I check with her later."

"I'll let her know you're looking for her, but I'm pretty sure she and Gordon are planning on leaving this evening."

I study the window again. It's a crank variety with an interior screen and is taller than I am. "Who discovered Todd's body?"

Brax picks up the brush. "Rhys." His skin takes on an ashen sheen as he remembers. "It was late and I was in my office, going over numbers again. He was in our bedroom."

On the first floor, it faces the backyard and gardens. "Saw the body as it went by and heard the..."

He doesn't need to finish. I can imagine the sound of the impact. Both our attentions slide to the outline. "How awful. When was the last time you opened that attic window?"

"In the spring when Rhys wanted to air it out. Place was filled with all kinds of old antique furniture and boxes of stuff Uphill had stored there. We got rid of most of it and organized the rest. Took me nearly an hour to pry it open. Damaged the paint on the ledge."

Preston Uphill was the previous owner, and a man who'd tried to kill me. I tried not to think about him. "Why on earth would Todd be in the attic?"

He starts scrubbing the wire rack. "Duh, Ava. To jump."

"His ghost says differently."

He stops. "Is he here now? What did he tell you?"

"He was around a few minutes ago, hovering near his fiancée and the detective. I couldn't exactly quiz him." I glance at the area, hoping the ghost might have followed, but all I see are plants wilting in the heat. "Each time he's spoken, he insists he would not take his own life."

Brax shakes his head and resumes his work. "This is bad, bad business."

He reminds me so much of his mother in that moment, I reach out and touch his shoulder. "I'm here for you."

He pats my hand. "I know."

"After it happened, was anything out of sorts there?"

"Nothing noticeable, but I was upset when Jones asked me the same thing and had me look around. The only thing that appeared disturbed was the window itself. The screen had been removed and set against an old chair, and obviously, it was open."

"Were you the one to find the note?"

"Gordon did. When we discovered what happened, he ran to Todd's room. He mentioned later to Jones that he thought the man had jumped from there."

Seemed peculiar to me that he would go to Todd's room, but in such an event, who knew how'd you respond? "And there was nobody else here? You're sure?"

He wipes sweat from his brow with the edge of his T-shirt. "I think I'd know if there had been." His tone comes out a little sharp, and he peers at me with an apologetic smile. I don't take offense and offer a return smile. He studies my face. "You look like Hades on a bad day."

My best friend doesn't pull punches. "Feel like it, too."

He draws me into a sweaty hug. "I'm here if *you* need anything. You know that, right?"

Accepting his embrace, I smile into his beefy bicep. "You just take care of Rhys."

We chat about the hot weather and Sage's party, ignoring the bright white outline on the ground a few feet away. Eventually, I head back home.

Neither Tabby nor Persephone are around, but I find Logan on the screened porch overlooking Aunt Willa's flower gardens. Birds sing lazily, bees fly around in a stupor and land here and there to gather pollen. Down the hill near the creek, I scan the old homestead to see if I spot Tabitha or my grandfather. I hear the faintest laughter and see a couple's shadow in an upstairs window. They appear to be kissing.

Samuel is a ghost, and I've forbidden my witchy grand-mother from bringing back his corporeal body, but somehow, the two can apparently enjoy each other anyway. I'm quite sure I don't want to know more.

The screen door screeches as it closes behind me, sounding a protest as if it's sick of the heat as well. The ceiling fans create a breeze, and Logan slides his readers off the end of his nose. He's on the loveseat, a stack of files next to him. "I still need to oil that hinge, don't I?"

"The least of our worries." I collapse into a chair, wiping a bead of sweat from my neck. I jut my chin toward the homestead. We've had the Quigbys working slowly but steadily on it for several months. The roof is new, as well as the siding. The sagging foundation has been shored up. Next are replacement windows. "Those two act more like honeymooners than you and I."

"We still have to plan that, as I recall. I hope we're the same after three hundred years."

"We also still have to plan our wedding." Technically we're married, after a handfasting ceremony in June, but his mother insists on a full-blown traditional ceremony this fall. "We're having dinner with your parents Wednesday."

"Great," he says with mock enthusiasm. "How was the tea party?"

"Lovely, but needs improvement, according to St. Helen." It's the nickname I privately call her. "She's emailing her list of suggestions to Sage this week. Speaking of, I need to get back over there. Sage is upset over the snake and that Zultan machine. It's spitting out prophecies left and right, after not working for weeks. She apparently saw a grim in her own tea leaves."

Logan simply stares at me. "I'm sorry. What?"

I explain, and he listens, a frown on his handsome face. "Could she be cursed?"

"After all you and I have seen, I wouldn't be surprised. Even so, Sage is smart and experienced with magic. She's known as the hex-breaker in her family. It's odd to see her unnerved by this."

He straightens and rests his elbows on his knees. "Lia was acting odd, too."

That's the next thing I explain. "Zultan freaked her out as well. That fortune teller is unusual, that's for sure."

"Want me to take a look at it? Sage must have misunderstood about it not functioning properly when she bought it. Or maybe it got jostled in the move to the shop and that caused it to work again."

"I went over it thoroughly and I'm baffled. It needs electricity, but there's no cord. It's been ripped out."

"As if someone wanted to make sure it didn't offer any fortunes again?"

Paranoia, or perhaps something worse, sends a shiver down my spine. I dig out my phone. "She needs to get rid of that thing. I'll talk to her."

Neither Bis, nor Raven, have replied to my messages, but Sage has sent me a text. *Going home. Talk tomorrow.*

So much for that. I decide not to press, and Logan stands and draws me over to the porch swing. We sit side-by-side and listen to the birds while he rocks us. I lay my head on his shoulder, thinking about Todd's ghost, but the heat and my tiredness get the best of me; I drift off.

When I wake later, my head is in Logan's lap on a pillow. He and Brax are speaking in soft tones. Yawning, I sit up. "How long was I out?"

Logan glances at his watch. "Half an hour. You were beat. Your mother phoned, by the way. Wants you to call her back. Said she would have come over, but she has her hands full with Queenie."

Brax and I exchange a look. "She's still worried to beat the band over what happened," he says.

The late afternoon sun shimmers through breaks in the trees, bathing the yard in peaches and pinks. "Why don't we go inside and cool off?"

Brax picks at his T-shirt. "I'm too grubby. Probably should grab a shower."

I shift to the edge of the swing. "I'll come over later and see if I can talk to the ghost again. I'm actually surprised he's transporting himself between here and the hospital. Usually earthbound spirits can't move away from their physical body more than five miles or so."

Logan begins collecting his piles of folders. "You never end up with a ghost who acts the way they're supposed to. Look at Sherlock."

"May we all be so rebellious when our time comes." Brax rises, fist bumps Logan, and says goodbye.

In the kitchen, I pour two glasses of iced sweet tea, and text Sage. *Let me know when you want to cleanse your shop. You should throw away that carnival game.*

Logan joins me and we clink glasses. "You should call Lia and check on her," he presses me. "She seemed really off when I dropped her at home."

I check the time, but I don't know when her movie marathon was supposed to begin, and I'm hoping she's out of her funk. If so, I don't want to remind her of today's events. "I'll check on her later. Right now, I better call Mama."

EIGHT

Mondays are normally slow at The Wedding Chapel. Thanks to the heatwave, I have no walk-ins and spend the morning catching up on paperwork. I find it difficult to concentrate, however, considering everything that's happened in the past twenty-four hours.

Tea Leaves is closed on Mondays, but I find myself routinely checking for Sage's car. She often does private readings, and I hope she'll appear.

Rosie, along with Jenn, my part-time employee, arrive in the afternoon, bringing their babies with them. I take a break to play with Avalene, named after myself and Helen, while Rosie checks orders. Jenn decorates the front windows with new displays of my dresses, while her daughter, Yasmine, naps.

Avalene coos on a mat in the corner of my office, Rosie's tiny Chihuahua, Fern, watching her with fascination. I bring out a pink and white striped box and open it. Inside is the christening gown I had Gloria, the seamstress and owner of

Miss Jasmine's Boutique Bridal Designs, sew from one of my sketches. Gloria's talent knows no bounds, and together, we've created a beautiful work of art.

I hold it up so Avalene can see it, and her dark eyes, complete with lashes I envy, widen. She kicks her legs and waves her hands, catching a piece of the lace skirt and trying to bring it to her mouth. Good enough for me. My namesake has put her stamp of approval on it, and that makes me ridiculously happy.

When Rosie finishes with a call, I repack the dress and take it and Avalene to her desk. I hand her the box. "Ava Junior loves it."

Her eyes, identical to the child's, also widen. She claps her hands in anticipation. "It's ready?"

"Since the christening is Saturday afternoon, I sure hope so." I jiggle the baby on my hip. It feels natural, and makes me think about one of my own. This is a new feeling for me, and it takes me off guard. "If you don't love it, I'll run to the boutique and find something else."

Rosie sets the box on her desk with reverence and slowly peels off the lid. She uncovers the dress under the tissue paper and her breath catches. Carefully, she lifts the garment and holds it up, the satin top shining in the light. A hand covers her mouth and tears flood her eyes. "Oh my stars, it's gorgeous."

"Only the best for my goddaughter." I knew she'd love it, but I'm still relieved. I kiss Avalene's nose. "There's a matching headband, but we both know this little stinker won't leave it on longer than a few seconds. I was hoping with the right distraction"—namely Logan, whom the baby adores—"we might be able to keep her in it long enough to get a couple pictures."

Rosie chuckles and Jenn brings Yasmine over to inspect the outfit. "Whoa, that's cool. This could be a whole new line of products." She fluffs the skirt. "I'm not even into this christening stuff and I want something special like this for Yazzy."

Rosie thoroughly examines the gown and nods enthusiastically. "That's actually an excellent idea, Jenn."

"Sure," I tell them, "in all my spare time, I can whip out a line of christening gowns."

We share some laughter, and the babies join in, babbling and gurgling. Fern comes to check out what's going on, and even my cats, Arthur and Lancelot, stroll in to make sure they aren't missing anything. They aren't magical in any way, which in my house, is unusual.

Later, when the girls are asleep and Rosie and Jenn are taking a break, I sneak my sketchpad from the bottom drawer of my desk and play with a couple designs. Using Avalene's creation as a starting point, I change the type of skirt and keep the accents simple. While the gown is important, it should never overshadow the child. I've seen elaborate pieces that make me cringe with the amount of beads and other potential choking hazards on them. It's something you don't think about when you don't have children of your own, but since being around my godchild and Yasmine, I now pay attention to such dangers.

By early evening, the women and children are gone and Bis brings Sage over while Logan and I are having a glass of wine. Bis is a thin fellow with a boy-next-door appearance and an easygoing personality. He can also see ghosts.

Sage is subdued. "I'm ready to do it," she announces. "Are you still willing to help?"

"Of course." I set down my glass and tug Logan from his seat on the couch. "What do you need us to do?"

"Us?" he echoes.

Bis gives him a knowing smile.

"I'm going to smudge and do a spell to remove any curses or unwanted entities," Sage says, and Bis puts an arm around her shoulder. She leans into him. "I prefer to have five people for it, but four will have to do."

My poor husband gives a sigh, clearly uncomfortable about his needed participation. He keeps hold of his beverage. "Can I bring my drink?"

"Good idea," Bis says. "Can I get one?"

Sage elbows him. "Don't joke. This is serious."

The two men sneak a glance at each other that says a shot of liquid courage is serious business, too. Logan heads to the kitchen. "I believe whiskey might be a better choice, Bis."

"I second that," he calls.

"Have you considered that Trysta left a bit of her mojo behind?" I ask Sage. The former renter, and my potential sister-in-law, was working blood magic into her cupcakes to entrap Logan's brother back in June.

She fingers her messenger bag's strap, lying across her chest. "During the remodel I checked for residuals and I didn't find any. When you destroyed the cupcakes, I think that took care of it."

"It was just a thought. Do you want me to grab Brax or Rhys for the fifth person?"

She chews her bottom lip, thinking it over. "They have enough on their plate right now. We can do this."

I agree. Logan comes back with a whiskey bottle and two shot glasses. "Okay, well,"—I motion at the door—"let's get this party started."

I don't miss the fact Logan also grabs the half full wine bottle and brings it with us. Since I find myself a bit apprehensive about returning to the shop, I might need some of that liquid courage myself.

Passing my office, I grab my tools, still packed from my Saturday night at the morgue.

As we're crossing the street, I notice my many-times great-grandmother, in human form and wearing one of my shirts and a pair of jean shorts, sitting at a café table. Seeing her this way is always a shock, but at least she has clothes on. Her preferred mode is to run around in her birthday suit, much to my embarrassment.

"Hear ye need another warm body." Her Scottish accent is lovely. "May I?"

Her beauty is unparalleled and, legs crossed, she swings one lazily. Anyone who didn't know her would believe she's barely forty. They certainly wouldn't consider her a witch.

The gleam in her eyes tells me how much she's hoping to work magic, and Sage seems delighted, the first smile I've seen in the past day brightening her face. "I'd be honored to have you join us."

While Sage smudges, Bis and Logan haul the Zultan machine to Bis' work truck. After we're finished here, they'll take the macabre thing to the city dump.

Tabitha and I scoot tables out of the way, and then she uses chalk to draw a hexagon on the floor. At the five points, I place crystals, and in the center, a black pillar candle.

When we're all gathered, my grandfather, Samuel, appears. He exchanges greetings with those of us who can see him, but he can't keep his eyes off my grandmother's legs. He's had a bit of trouble adjusting to how things are now, since he died in the early 1800s, yet is doing better than expected, thanks to her.

She winks and stares boldly back at him through lowered eyelashes. We all try to ignore their flirting, but it's a bit of a challenge.

Persephone also appears, her on-again, off-again boyfriend, Sherlock, with her.

He believes he's the real character, and even dresses as him. Since he's good at solving mysteries, I've found him to be useful. Besides, I rather like him. More so than my guardian angel on most days. Their romance has been so rocky, I can't keep track of whether they're getting along or not, but since their fingers are entwined, I assume things are copacetic for now. "The Zultan machine is talking," Sherlock tells me.

"Out in my truck?" Bis is incredulous, and I have to explain to the others what he's announced. By the look on each of their faces, Bis is not alone in his shock.

Persephone nods. Sherlock adjusts his glasses and appears circumspect. "Is the thing possessed?"

"It has to be," I say, "but I can't detect any spirit in or near it. Would you be willing to check it out?"

Persephone starts to argue, but Sherlock looks thrilled. "Yes, of course. I'll do that now."

He vanishes, and, after giving me a scowl, Persephone disappears as well.

"Beautiful day for magic," Tabitha says.

It is now that my crabby spirit guide is gone. If I have another chance to speak to Sherlock, maybe I can put him on the trail of Todd's ghost and see what we can uncover.

Sage positions us around the outside of the hexagon, lights the candle, and away we go. It's a simple, straightforward spell, and although Logan and Bis are both uneasy, we are finished before either can down a shot of whiskey.

"Perhaps you should weave your magic into the walls," my grandmother tells Sage. "An added layer of protection for ye."

My friend considers it. "I regularly refresh my magical boundaries of the entire property, and I've had the place blessed."

This is news to Logan. "What kind of blessing?"

"One by Reverend Stout, and a second by a high priestess."

Logan seems impressed. "How can the place be cursed then, or allow anything that is, in?"

Tabitha begins listing all kinds of ways such things can occur. "By binding ye magic to the place," she explains to Sage, "the building becomes an extension of ye. It will be able to act on its own to keep out evil entities."

Sage glances at me, then away. "Can you show me?"

My grandmother beams, always ready to do more magic. "I would love to."

Tabitha pulls Sage aside and Sherlock returns. "Sorry, but I can find no spirit inside the mannequin or attached to the machine's parts," he tells me.

"Thanks for checking." I give Logan and Bis the go ahead and they leave for the landfill with it.

"Say, Sherlock, would you be able to help me with—"

"No." Persephone materializes and cuts me off. "We're busy."

Before I can continue about Todd, they disappear.

I hold in my sigh and grab the bottles of liquor. Keeping my nose out of the witchy business, I return to The Wedding

Chapel, print off the contract for the November birthday party, and march over to the B&B.

"Is Jill around?" I ask Rhys.

Like usual, he's in the kitchen, cooking. "Upstairs, I believe. Why?"

I flash the paper. "Hoping to get this signed before she and her husband take off."

"They've decided to stay until Wednesday." His cheeks are flushed from the heat of whatever is on the stove. "They bought our August special, just like Todd. It's been really slow the last few weeks, everyone getting ready for back-to-school, I guess. I was hoping we could fill all four rooms, but ended up with only two. I heard Miss Dixie is petitioning the City Council and Chamber of Commerce to hold a peanut festival next year at this time. It could bring in a lot more business."

Mama is always coming up with ideas to bolster tourism and support our town. "The Peaches and Peanuts Festival." I've heard all about it. "It's sure to be a hit. You'll be booked that week for sure."

He motions to the floor above us. "The Carrs are in 221B Baker Street."

I lift a brow. "A Sherlock room?"

Our friendly ghost detective recently upset Rhys and I had to intervene and negotiate a truce. Sherlock meant no harm, but he was freaking out my friend with some of his invisible maneuvers.

"Yes, and there's Out Of Africa Safari and Magical Fairy Oasis. The fourth bedroom I've left as good ol' southern charm. I call it the Sweet Tea and Slumber Room."

"You're brilliant."

He grins. "I like to think so."

"Does Sherlock know?"

"I haven't noticed him around, except for a calabash that appeared out of the blue the day after I hung the sign on the wall next to the room. It was lying on the bed when I went to put on fresh linens."

I chuckle. "I hope you don't mind."

"Nah." He wipes his hands on a towel. "As long as he doesn't disturb the guests, or fiddle with my things, he can visit."

"Is Brax at The Thorny Toad?"

"Not tonight. I'm bartending, though." He glances at the clock over the table and turns off the stove. "Better get a move on." He takes the soup pan off the burner, sets it on a nearby cooling rack, and removes his apron, hanging it on a hook next to the back door. "You should come by. We've got a new psychic, Madam X. She's from Romania and her specialty is palm reading. She's really good."

Madam X? *Really?* I give him a *maybe next time* smile. "I think I've had about all the messages from the beyond I can handle for one day."

NINE

R hys narrows his eyes at me, but doesn't ask for details. He lowers his voice. "I need a break from here. Everyone, including me, is on edge." He glances past my shoulder to the open doorway to make sure we're still alone before continuing in that covert voice. "Truthfully, I'm surprised the Carrs are staying. They were totally rattled last night, and Gordon has stayed in that room all day. It's like he's afraid he'll run into Todd's ghost or something."

That *is* a possibility. "It's a lot to take in, but I'm glad they stayed. I'll run this up to Jill and then be off."

I hesitate outside their closed door when I overhear her and Gordon arguing in hushed tones.

"We need to leave," he says.

"Not until we're sure," she replies.

"It's not here. I told you, I checked everything."

She sighs as if speaking to an obstinate child. "We need to look again. We have to destroy it."

"If he even had such a thing, it's fake. I'm sure of it."

"What if it isn't? What if he gave it to *her*? Maybe she knows."

The mattress springs creak from the weight of somebody sitting on it.

"She doesn't know or she would have said something. One more day," he insists. "I'll make sure she doesn't have it, and then we're gone."

The whole discussion makes the hairs on my arms rise. They must be referring to Todd, but what did he have, or *not* have, that they're worried about?

I turn the conversation over in my mind, the Carrs now silent. Jill claimed they didn't know Todd, yet it seems they may have. I contemplate retreating and coming back later, but my feet are glued to the floor.

Waiting, I keep hoping they'll resume their discussion and give me something more. I consider running home to grab my phone, which has an app for recording audio, but I'm afraid I might miss something important while I'm gone.

"How long do you think she'll hang around?" Jill asks. "It would be wise for us to wait until she leaves."

Again, my curiosity is piqued. I turn my head to bring my ear closer to the wood. Down the hall, I notice the entry to the safari room is cracked open.

"Why are you being so stubborn?" Gordon's heavy footsteps make the floorboards creak. Jill must be the one on the bed. "I couldn't care less how long she remains in this ridiculous place. I need to get home and figure out our next step. I can't do that here. And you certainly can't be throwing a party in November. What is wrong with you?"

I frown.

"If you weren't always trying to get ahead," she rants fiercely, voice rising, "we could have handled this quietly."

"You're blaming me?"

Before she responds, an orange blur jets past my feet and plops down on her haunches. "*Meow*," Tabby screeches, giving me an innocent look with her gold colored eyes.

The heavy footsteps draw closer. I make a face and step back a heartbeat before the door swings open. Tabby races down the hall to the safari room, slipping inside.

Gordon glares at me. "What are you doing here?"

I hold up the paper. "I need Jill to sign this. It's for the party."

He looks me over from head to toe, ignoring the contract. "Were you listening to us?"

I do my best to appear indignant. "I was chasing my cat." I point down the hall. Luckily, she pokes her head out at that moment, then disappears inside once more. "Don't tell Rhys, okay? She's not supposed to be in here. Anyway, if I could get Jill's signature, I'll make a copy of this and email it to her."

Coming up behind him, she peeks over his shoulder. "How kind. You didn't have to bring that over."

I paste on a wide smile as her husband's face goes red and he turns away. "We are full-service. I wanted you to have it before you left. You're sure you didn't know Todd?"

Gordon has his back to us, facing the window that over-looks the front yard and street. I see his fists clench.

"Never met him or Sandra before," Jill claims. My father, once a police officer with Thornhollow PD, has taught me how to watch people's faces for signs they're lying. When she says it, she glances to the left and shifts her weight ever so slightly. "I'm sure he is—*was*—a very nice person."

Uh huh. "I'm sure he was." I peer down the hallway. "I was hoping to talk to Sandra. Have you seen her?"

Jill snatches the paper from my hand. "She's around somewhere. We are, of course, giving her space."

"I didn't see her car out front."

"I left it at the church." The click of heels sound on the wooden steps leading to the third floor. A pair of gray shoes comes into view. Step by step, we see Sandra's legs, then the rest of her. Her eyes are still red and swollen, but she appears calmer. "Your minister was kind enough to speak to me and offer support."

If I play my cards right, getting all three of them in one spot to talk could help me figure things out. "Reverend Stout is a source of strength for all of us," I say, a bit too cheerily. "I'm glad he could help you." I wonder why she's been in the attic. I guess she needed to see Todd's final view, as morbid as that seems to me. "Are you staying long?"

I don't see so much as sense the Carrs stiffening.

"Rhys has been a doll and offered to let me keep the reservation Todd made through Wednesday. I thought I might at least spend tonight here."

I feel terrible for her. "Can I get you anything?"

She strolls toward the safari room. "Some peace would be nice."

Taking the hint, I nod. "As soon as I get my cat out of there, I'll leave you be."

"That's not what I meant." She places a hand over her heart. "Peace in here. I can't accept that he's gone, and I don't believe for one minute he jumped from that window."

Tabby races from the room, past all of us, disappearing down the steps. Sandra lowers her chin and enters, shutting the door quietly behind her.

I give the Carrs a parting smile and follow Tabby. Sandra isn't the only one with doubts.

By the time I hit the veranda, the sun is setting and I'm determined to call Detective Jones and voice my suspicions. He'll laugh and once more tell me to stay out of it. I have nothing concrete.

Sage catches me as I'm entering my yard. There's color in her cheeks and she's smiling. "Rhys says we need to go to The Toad tonight."

"I take it the spell went well?"

"Your grandmother is so powerful. An amazing witch. I'm surprised you didn't inherit more of her magic."

"Probably a good thing I didn't. You go on and have fun. I have other things to do."

Persephone appears on the top step, blocking my way. "Go with Sage."

I walk through her, shivering at the frigid feel of it. *Not right*, my body says, even though she's not a ghost. "I can't," I say, letting myself into the house. Thankfully, the gargoyles are silent. Tabby moseys in with me. "I have to dig deeper into Todd's death."

"Your friend needs you more than he does at the moment," she argues. Her chandelier earrings are so long they brush her shoulders. "You need to go."

She disappears.

"Your cryptic messages are not helpful," I yell at the ceiling.

An hour later, Sage, Bis, Logan, and I are at The Thorny Toad, about to be wowed by Madam X and her ability to read our palms.

TEN

The Toad is hopping. Brax and Rhys recently moved the metaphysical hangout from the old ironworks building outside of town to the former floral shop a few blocks from the B&B. Because they own multiple businesses, it made sense for them to have this one closer.

The two-story Victorian provides the perfect atmosphere for the booths of psychics, energy workers, and astrologists on the second floor, while the first is a great place for folks to just hang out, have a drink, and share ideologies and philosophies.

Tonight's music coming from the overhead speakers is a combination of flutes, wind chimes, and drum beats. Soothing, yet upbeat.

Sage inhales deeply and sighs. The place typically smells like patchouli and lavender. "I love it here."

Betty, the former owner, cleared the interior walls below for her floral shop while she lived upstairs. Trailing house plants still decorate the space, along with dozens of books, candles, and pretty packages of Queenie's latest selection of candies.

At the rear of the room is the bar. Formerly Betty's workstation, Brax and Rhys replaced her counter with their scarred, thick wooden top from the old Toad. The flower coolers have become refrigeration units for the food they serve.

Rhys dances behind the bar, creating a fruity drink for a woman sitting there. Her companion has a beer. When Rhys spots us, he waves us over.

The four of us stick to ginger ale and fizzy water, and Rhys seems to delight in decking the glasses with fruit garnishes. He's definitely out of his funk. "I'm so glad you came," he says, setting them on orange napkins. "These are on the house."

"You can't give away your inventory," I chastise.

He makes shooing motions. "Go put your name down for a reading with Madam X. There's a waiting list, so while you're hanging, buy some of Queenie's candies and maybe a card deck or a candle." He winks at Sage. "I just put out new tarot sets I think you'll like."

She hustles in the direction that he points, making a squealing noise. Bis rolls his eyes good-naturedly and follows.

Logan takes a folded bill out of his back pocket and sticks it in Rhys' tip jar. My friend winks at him, and we go to see about getting in line for Madam X.

"You can't seriously want her to read your palm," Logan says, as I scratch our names on a small tablet decorated with moons and stars outside her closed door. We are second, and I'm relieved, since I'm tired and want to go to bed.

Sage, like Rhys, seems to be feeling better, and for the

life of me, I don't know why Persephone insisted we come with her tonight, but I'd like to wrap this up quickly. "It's important to our friends, so yes, I'm going to let this woman read my palm."

He leans in and nuzzles my ear, making me giggle. "You do a lot for everybody else, you know that? They're lucky to have you."

I finish and we gravitate to the end of the hall near a giant window, not that much different than the B&B's. The rear lot is small, due to the fact Betty turned most of it into parking spots, but Brax and Rhys have strung tiny lights along the porch railing, and placed solar ones along a path that leads to a bench. It contrasts with the asphalt, but adds a nice ambience.

There's a couple on the bench, kissing, and it makes me smile. "If that's true, why is it I feel as if I'm letting others down? I didn't get Avenger to pass to the afterlife, and I haven't figured out what happened with Todd. There's definitely something fishy going on with his death."

I relay the conversation I overheard between the Carrs to Logan, as well as the fact they deny knowing Todd. His brow furrows. "Suspicious, but not damning. What do you think they're trying to find?"

I draw my phone from my purse. "No clue. I'm going to text Jones and voice my concerns."

Madam X's client leaves, looking sort of stunned. The palm reader is dressed in a flowing purple gown with a crocheted burgundy colored shawl, a matching wrap around her head that reminds me of Zultan, and chandelier earrings not much different than Persephone's. She murmurs something heavily accented to the aging woman as she escorts her to the stairs, and the gal nods absentmindedly.

.70   NYX HALLIWELL

"It's not much to go on," Logan says. "I doubt he'll be receptive to your butting in."

"He absolutely won't be." I finish the message and send it. "But I added a teaser that might make him take me seriously."

Her client disappears, and Madam X checks the notebook, calling out for her next client.

"Todd's spirit?" Logan murmurs.

Although he says it too quietly for her to hear over the music and conversations filtering up from the lower floor, she turns in our direction. Her face is free of wrinkles, but I'm sure she's over fifty. "You must be Avalon," she says in that accented voice. "Please come in. Your friend..." She glances over the railing, scanning the room below. "Where is she?"

Logan and I exchange a look. "We aren't the next on your list," he says.

She waves him off, a stack of crystal bracelets clinking together. "I will speak to you first." Her eyes slide to me and away. "You and the witch. I've been waiting for you. I have a message for you."

Not too ominous. Maybe Rhys told her I might be stopping in, and perhaps he mentioned Sage, too. Or, there was the possibility that Madam X was a true psychic and Persephone had contacted her. Either way, my skin crawls. She has a message for me, all right, and I'm pretty sure I don't want it.

Bis and Sage climb the steps, Madam X spreading her arms wide in welcome. "There you are," she says to Sage. "I sensed your energy as soon as you entered. We have a lot to discuss."

Sage is holding a deck of cards, but something in the

psychic's expression makes her drop them. "It's true then, isn't it?"

"This is going to be about as much fun as being interrogated by Detective Jones," I say under my breath.

Logan snorts and gives my hand a squeeze. "Want me to get you a stronger drink?"

There's no alcohol on the planet strong enough for me at the moment. "Let's just get this over with."

The two of us start forward, and Bis picks up the box. Madam X takes Sage by the arm and directs her inside. She waves me in, but puts up a hand to stop Logan and Bis. "Ladies only," she says, and shuts the door in their astonished faces.

With a flurry of her arm, she directs us to a table. Logan, not one to have doors slammed on him, flings it open. "Ava decides, not you."

I love this man.

Not all psychics are witches, but my first thought is, *don't piss off Madam X*. "It's okay," I assure him as she gives him the stink eye. "Could you wait for us downstairs?"

He's not happy and pauses a moment, but eventually nods, and they leave.

Once the door is shut again, I glance at Sage. She's far too pale and her fingers twitch. I reach over and take her hand. "You're safe, and I'm right here. This is just for fun."

"I understand you're the most powerful witch in town," Madam X says. She tugs my grip from Sage's. "With great power comes great adversity. I see it in your aura, a darkness. You have your affairs in order, yes?"

"Oh, for heaven's sake." I stand and start to pull Sage up. "There is no darkness in her aura, and we didn't come here for doom and gloom. I thought you were a legit palm reader."

She turns dark eyes on me. "Sit, Avalon. There is much I need to tell both of you."

My bravado falters. What if Sage *is* cursed? Is that why Persephone insisted I come? I let go a mental swear that would make Mama cringe.

"Please, Ava," Sage urges in a quiet voice. "I can't run from fate. Better to prepare for it."

Madam X seems to not care whether I stay or not, but I refuse to leave my friend alone with her. I sink into the chair once more.

"Palms are portals into great insight." Madam X takes Sage's hand. One ringed finger traces a line. "Strong life line, but short. You may meet with illness and disease before old age. Fate is..." She glances up and Sage goes even paler. "Your fate is strongly connected to your love line."

Sage visibly swallows.

The woman scans her aura. "There is a mysterious man in your life. Heed his warnings."

"Zultan," Sage whispers, flicking a glance at me. "I told you he was for real."

Pressing my lips together, I count to five. Then ten. "He's a carnival act, Sage. A mannequin."

Madam X releases her. "The fortune teller?"

Sage nods. "Could his predictions be true? I saw a grim in my tea leaves, too." She scrubs a hand over her eyes. "Am I going to die soon?"

Nothing changes in the psychic's expression. "Perhaps."

"That's it." I jump to my feet. "We're done."

"You would be wise to guard your own fate," Madam X tells me. "Many of the dead hover around you."

That's as accurate as anything she's claimed so far, yet no ghost is within spitting distance. "And you would be wise to stop scaring innocent people. Come on." I grab Sage's arm and physically haul her from the room.

"Be careful, Avalon," Madam X calls after us. "Or you'll be joining the dead soon."

Downstairs, I gather the men, tell Rhys to put the deck of tarot cards on my bill, and hustle everyone out. Sage is a zombie, and Bis is clearly concerned. "What happened?" he asks.

"Everyone back to our place," is all I'll say.

When we arrive, I make Sage down two shots of Logan's whiskey. "Do not put stock in what that woman said," I tell her.

Her eyes are sad when they meet mine. "I have to. Don't you see? There are too many omens all saying the same thing."

"What?" Bis demands.

"I'm going to die soon," she replies deadpanned, detached. Numb. "It's my fate."

"Fate is a word for giving your power away to outside influences. You and I know that every decision and action has a consequence." I poke the table with a finger. "We determine our fate. Not others."

"Stop being stubborn, Ava."

Her tone sets me back a step. "Stop being suckered into some ridiculous belief."

Her eyes harden. "You know it's true. You're in denial because you're scared. I am, too, but that won't change the outcome." She slams the shot glass down. "By the way, your tea leaves the other day were skull and crossbones."

Well, that can't be good. "What does it mean?"

"Danger is in your path." She walks away and both men glance at me with stunned expressions.

"Wait," I call, following her to the door. "Whatever is going on, I'll figure it out." I know she's right—all these omens are pointing to one outcome, and I have no explanation for them. "I need to talk to Persephone and my grandmother. Don't do anything until I get back to you."

She pauses with her hand on the doorknob. She is equal parts resigned and resentful. "There's nothing they can do. Nothing you can do. I have to go."

"Stay here." I mean it as an offer, but it sounds like a command. "If you're truly in danger, let us protect you."

"Don't you get it? There's nothing you can do to stop this from happening."

Bis joins us and reaches for her arm. "Babe, maybe Ava's right."

She jerks away. "Don't call me that, and don't follow me. I want to be alone."

She storms out, leaving the three of us stunned and unsure of what to do.

Logan places his hand on my lower back, supportive. "Give her some breathing space."

Bis looks as shell shocked as I feel. "Is she really going to die?"

I close the door, leaning against it and feeling like I've lost a friend. Not due to any omen, but because Sage is correct—I'm scared. I didn't listen to her and tried to override her fears by convincing myself it was all hogwash.

"Not if I can help it," I say quietly, and then I put out an SOS to my guardian angel, my grandmother, and the other spirits I know—Samuel and Sherlock. "Between the living and the dead, we're going to save her."

ELEVEN

Since Bis can see and hear spirits like me, I only need to interpret for Logan what they say during our meeting.

My grandmother, however, places a spell on him that temporary gives him "the sight" as she calls it, and allows him to hear the conversation.

"Knowing the date of someone's demise is above my pay grade," Persephone tells us. She's wearing a slinky blue pantsuit and sticking close to Sherlock. He stares into the dormant fireplace as if it holds the answers we seek. "I have no idea if these warnings should be heeded."

Real helpful. "Any chance you could trade me for her?" While Persephone is often challenging, the idea of not having her around to help me is unnerving. I'm willing to do it if she can save my friend. "Can you be her guardian angel until we understand what we're up against?"

"I wish it were that simple. I'm assigned to you, and until I get divine orders otherwise, you're stuck with me."

I pinch the bridge of my nose. "Can you at least counsel her?"

"I doubt she'll listen, but I can try. It will probably fall on deaf ears."

My attempts have, but I'm not a guardian angel, nor have I been a good friend. "What about the boundary magic you did?" I ask Tabitha. "Is there any other protection spell we can layer over that to keep her safe?"

"Many," she answers. She and Samuel sit side-by-side on the sofa, while I pace and Logan watches me from his chair. "Ye be needing to know the source of the danger, though, to protect her properly."

"You cannot simply protect her from everything," Samuel explains. "Not effectively. We need a starting place to understand where the threat comes from."

Tabitha nods. "With that knowledge, I can weave a successful spell around her, and infuse charms with powerful magic to repel that which tries to harm her."

"It's my understanding," Sherlock says quietly without looking at us, "that when it's your time to go, it's your time to go. There's no magic—or anything else—that can prevent that."

I point at Tabitha. "She's living proof that's not true."

He glances her way. "She's an exception."

Boy, is she. "It *can* be done." I continue pacing. "How do we learn who or what this threat is? Is it human? A ghost? A curse?"

"Begin with the obvious. Does she have any enemies?" Logan asks, looking at Bis.

He spreads his hands wide. "I don't know of any. There are people in town who don't like that she's a witch. Your mother's approval of the tea house seems to have put a damper on any blatant hatred toward her, though."

On her worst days, Sage is disinterested, and occasionally, short tempered. She doesn't go out of her way to make friends, yet, she doesn't ruffle feathers either. I scan my memories, attempting to think of somebody who's seemed hateful or offended by her. I come up blank.

"People lash out against those they fear," my grandmother says. "Could it be someone who is afraid of magic itself? Who believes witches as a whole are evil?"

"Possibly." Those who know Sage knows she's powerful, but she never uses it for her own benefit or to hurt another. "But I don't know anybody specifically."

Bis echoes my thoughts. "She's gone out of her way to make sure people know she abides by the 'do no harm' rule. They have nothing to fear from her. She's about as evil as Reverend Stout."

Even he likes her. "I agree, but not everyone knows her as we do. They know *of* her, but this is a small town with a lot of old-fashioned views. Certain people give me the side-eye because they've heard I'm a medium, and because Aunt Willa didn't hide her abilities. She was at The Thorny Toad at least once a month, giving readings, and did plenty of back door spellwork. I have a ledger with items and exchanges she did for various residents in this town over the years. She may not have hung a sign around her neck that said 'witch,' but she wasn't exactly in the magical closet."

For the first time since the beginning of our discussion, Sherlock perks up. "Did your aunt have any enemies? Someone who didn't care for her psychic abilities?"

"The only ones I know of are no longer around." Thank goodness. "Why? What are you thinking?"

He faces me, tugging on the end of his vest. "As you said, you are a medium, and you've assisted certain people with curses and hauntings, but you haven't exactly stepped into your aunt's shoes in the psychic field. Sage is openly a witch, filling the void your aunt left. She may be the target of those who feel she is a threat to their business."

"Like the psychics who work at The Toad?"

"They're all from out of town, though," Logan reminds me. "Most make a circuit of the area each week, don't they?"

"It's still a possibility." I stop pacing. "I might be able to learn who appreciated Aunt Willa's magic if I decode the ledger, but that won't point to anyone who might dislike Sage moving into town and taking up where she left off."

Logan sits forward. "Do you still have it?"

"Yes, of course. Why?"

"Just a hunch. Mind if I look through it?"

Persephone is nodding. "You might be on the right track. Process of elimination."

I hustle upstairs and retrieve the ledger from my aunt's trunk. After returning to hand it to Logan, he takes it to his office and closes the door.

"Is it feasible someone didn't care for a reading that she gave them?" I ask. "That seems more likely to me."

The others cast glances around, and Tabitha comments. "Disgruntled clients are a possibility."

"Bis, has she mentioned anyone being upset about what she told them?"

He shrugs. "One or two, but she hasn't been open that long. Most folks just come in for tea and a snack. I don't know any who would go to all this trouble to get back at her, and it's not as if she's making stuff up. She reads what's there. It's not her fault if their kid is going to fail calculus, or their current love interest is leaving them in three months."

Danger is in your path. Great.

I shove the worry aside. Sage has told me that the majority of her readings are women wanting to know about love and relationships. Definitely a touchy subject. One of them could be that upset. "How do we get a list of her dissatisfied customers? Does she keep track of who she does readings for?"

"Probably. She's the most organized person I know."

"Would she keep it at the shop? A ledger, perhaps, like my aunt's? Receipts or a journal?"

His brow creases when he frowns. "She has a small purple notebook in her purse all the time. I thought it was to write down spells when they come to her, but she definitely keeps track of names and dates. I've seen her reviewing them. Could that be her personal clients?"

Odds were, yes. Problem was, if it was in her bag, I had no chance of getting hold of it right now. I shoot off a message to her anyway, telling her our theory and asking her to bring it to me, along with any knowledge she had about those upset over her tea leaf interpretations.

I didn't need psychic abilities to tell me to expect the cold shoulder, and as the night wears on and we run out of ideas, I'm right—she doesn't respond.

Later in bed, I toss and turn wondering if we'll wake tomorrow and find her dead. *Stop it!*

I try to wipe the idea from my thoughts, and hate that our last spoken words to each other were harsh. I should have taken her seriously and given her unconditional support, rather than trivializing her fear.

At four, I tiptoe out of the room and head downstairs,

Arthur and Lancelot trailing after me in hopes of an early breakfast.

The deck of tarot cards Sage picked out sits on my desk. They have a lovely artwork with a dragonfly theme. I open the package and shuffle, having no idea what I'm doing but feeling the urge to use them. Persephone pops in, easing into the chair across from my desk. "Can't sleep?"

"With my friend in danger? I can barely stop myself from tracking her down and winding her up in bubble wrap." I shuffle again. "How do I do this?"

"There are various methods. The whole point is to let your intuition guide you. You don't need directions, you need to trust your magic. Do what feels right."

I don't have magic. That's the thing. "Madam X told Sage her fate was connected to her love line. I have a hard time believing that woman is a credible source, but is it possible Bis is a threat?"

Persephone fiddles with an earring. "Highly doubtful."

The Lovers card jumps out of my hands and lands on the surface. I glance at my guardian angel. "Is this a confirmation that he is or isn't?"

The corner of her mouth quirks in a grin. "What do you think?"

Her answers are always frustrating. "My gut tells me Bis isn't a danger to her." The couple on the card are staring into each other's eyes with their palms touching. A dragonfly sits on their fingertips. "If anything, he's more protective of her. I can see her breaking his heart, but not the other way around, and I know he would never physically harm her."

"Could it be that someone is using Sage to get at him?"

"That's a possibility I hadn't considered. But Bis? He's as well liked by the town as Mama."

"Perhaps Madam X isn't truly psychic, or was picking up on another who loves Sage."

"Like her sister?"

"I don't know anything about palm reading, but why not? Maybe Raven has an enemy who's going after Sage."

That seemed more fitting than the Bis angle. My shuffling gets faster as the cards become less stiff. "I don't like Madam X, nor do I trust her. My guess is that your first assumption is correct—she's *not* psychic."

"She does live in town, unlike the other Toad performers."

I stop. "That's right. She moved here recently."

"Ten days ago." Her eyes are burning a hole in me, as if this is important.

I tap the cards on the desktop and another jumps from my hand. The Moon.

It's pretty with a dragonfly spotlighted by a full moon behind it. The insect hangs upside down under a leaf, nearly invisible. "What does this mean?"

"Secrets, illusions, deception."

Representing Madam X?

Persephone is still staring at me with that look suggesting I'm onto something. "Can you believe that fake accent?" she asks.

I study her. "She's not Romanian?"

"Have you ever heard one that sounded like that?"

"Believe it or not, we don't have very many of them running around Thornhollow."

"You lived and worked in Atlanta for years, didn't you?"

"I wouldn't know a Romanian accent from a Russian one. Where is she originally from?"

"Good question. You might look into that. Another, if I can offer, is why did she come *here?*"

Without realizing I'm shuffling again, I glance down to see the Five of Wands on top. I hold it up.

"Rivalry, conflict, sowing discord."

If the cards are answering my questions, then... "She wasn't getting along with someone where she lived previously, so she left and came here. Is she still sowing discord?"

"She certainly upset you, as well as Sage. She wasn't the only thing that instigated your squabble with your friend, but she brought it to a head."

My next question is directed at the cards. "Is Sage in danger from Madam X?"

I shuffle, and shuffle some more. No card jumps out, and I don't feel a tug to stop. "Why won't they answer?"

"Try rephrasing the question."

I sigh wearily. "Is Madam X a threat to Sage?"

Still nothing.

"Oh, for heaven's sake." I slam them down and sit back. "This is pointless. The only person Madam X has truly threatened, albeit in a cryptic manner, is me."

This gets Persephone's undivided attention. "What did she say?"

"Nothing."

"Ava, tell me."

Giving in, I keep my voice unconcerned. "She said I need to be careful or I'll be joining the dead soon."

Persephone's spine goes ramrod straight and she comes out of the seat. "How dare she." She walks to the window, stomps back to the desk. "I may not know when other peoples' lives are up, but I do have an invested interest in yours. Now is not your time, I guarantee that."

A gentle breeze flows across my face. *Avalon.*

It's my aunt's voice. I can't see her, but I hear her speaking to me when she visits. I straighten, glancing around. "Aunt Willa?"

Persephone seems to spot her, her attention settling next to my right shoulder. My aunt doesn't answer verbally. Instead, a card flies from the deck and lands on the floor.

It's upside down and I get up to retrieve it.

"What is it?" Persephone asks.

My stomach drops. "Guess Madam X is right," I say, holding it up.

Persephone blanches and a hand goes to her chest. "No."

"Yep." I flip it onto the desk.

A dragonfly on its back with its feet in the air stares at me. No interpretation needed.

Death has arrived.

TWELVE

Persephone hurries to reassure me that the card does not represent physical death. The meaning is interpreted as an ending, a transition.

Right. My gut says it's no metaphor in this case. Even Aunt Willa is warning me. "I saw your reaction. If anything is ending, it's me."

Her arguments are half-hearted and eventually she leaves when I tell her I don't want to hear it.

I wait until six to call my dad. Mama answers their landline, but she's in a hurry to get in the shower because she has a breakfast meeting with the Zoning Commission. "Are you all right?" she asks. "You sound weird."

"I am weird," I remind her. "I was hoping Daddy could do me a favor."

"Ava, what's going on?"

"Nothing, Mama. I'm fine."

"I may not have my sister's gift of knowing, but I *am* your mother, and I know when something's wrong. My stomach has been a mess for the past two hours."

Telling my mother about my possible impending demise doesn't seem like the type of information you say over the phone. Or at all. "I'm just concerned about my friends. Events are...upsetting right now."

"Queenie has been worrying herself silly. I keep telling her we'll all get through this. The B&B will be just fine. Listen, I've got to run, but you know I love you. Don't do anything dumb, take your vitamins, and call me tonight, okay?"

The best of Dixie Fantome advice. "I love you, too."

Daddy comes on the line a minute later. "Mornin'. You're up early."

"Could you run a background check for me? There's a new psychic in town. I've got a feeling about her."

"The Fantome gut. It's never wrong. What's her name?"

"I don't know her real one. She goes by Madam X."

"Where's she from?"

"Not sure about that either. She claims she's Romanian, but that's part of her stage act."

"Okay..."

"I know that's not much to go on."

"That's pretty much nothing to go on."

"But the incredible skills of former Detective Nash Fantome are unbeatable."

"Flattery will get you everywhere."

I smile. "Thank you, Daddy."

We disconnect, and I do an internet search, in case she's used that moniker previously. An email from Dr. Ernestine dings my inbox. She wants to know if I had success evicting the ghost haunting the morgue.

Ugh. I put my head on my desk for a moment, before I respond. *Sorry*, I type. *I was interrupted and can't be sure*

*he crossed over. I can come back and check. If not, I'll try
again.*

Just as I'm sending that off, Logan enters. He kisses the
top of my head. "Insomnia again?"

"Did I keep you awake?"

"Not at all, but I'm worried about you. Are you okay?"

"Peachy," I lie.

"That's the spirit." He winks—a joke. "Coffee?"

"Yes, please."

The morning's news doesn't make good conversation
with your husband over breakfast. However, I start to tell
him what happened with the tarot cards, and find I can't get
the words out.

His mental attention is on a meeting he has. "I haven't
decoded all those names in the ledger yet, but I'll get on
them again tonight."

"It's a dead end," I tell him. "Don't worry about it."

"Are you sure?"

I nod. "What's important is that I make up with Sage
today."

This seems to relieve his mind. "She's a good friend, and
she's helped you out of several binds. You were both upset
yesterday, but I would hate for you to let it come between
you permanently."

My toast seems as dry as cardboard in my mouth. I
swallow it down with a big gulp of coffee. What will I say to
her? My perspective has definitely changed in the last twelve
hours. For both of us.

As Logan digs into his eggs and biscuits, I find I
can't eat anymore. I'm about to tell him about the Death
card when I hear the front door open. I left it unlocked
after taking Moxley for an early morning pee, and

wonder if Mama or Daddy have come by. "Hello?" I call.

Sage appears, face gaunt and white as a sheet. "Ava?"

I'm out of my seat and hugging her before she can say another word. "I'm sorry. I was out of line yesterday. Tell me what I can do to help."

She returns my hug. "I have a problem."

I step back and Logan and I give her a questioning look. She has a *big* problem, but we already know that. "Something else has happened?" he asks warily.

She sucks in a deep breath, closes her eyes briefly, then flips them open. Her hands are shaking. "You're not going to believe it."

"Sage?" I grab her hand and squeeze. "What is it?"

Her lips tremble. "It's...*Zultan*." She chokes on his name. "He's back."

Logan comes to his feet and we follow her, speechless. Moxley ambles behind as we cross the street and Sage motions us around to the side of the Tea Leaves building.

"Tabitha had me infuse the property with protection, so I guess he couldn't pass the boundary." She points to the machine, which now sits outside the edge of the rear parking lot staring at the building.

"How is that possible?" I take a step toward it and Logan grabs my arm.

"Don't touch it." He takes his phone out and shoots off a text. "It didn't get back here by itself, and it may have our culprit's prints on it. I want it dusted."

"This is out of hand. Whoever is doing this is making passive-aggressive threats to intimidate you," I say to Sage. "I'm notifying Detective Jones."

The machine comes to life, making a whirring noise. The

mannequin swivels his head, his blank gaze landing on me. "Come closer. Zultan will tell all."

The slot below kicks out a card. My feet are moving before my brain engages in an effort to keep whatever message is on it from Sage.

I'm halfway to it when my husband stops me again. His blue eyes are fierce. "We wait for my guy."

"You know someone who can lift fingerprints?"

He points toward The Wedding Chapel, turning me around and marching me toward it. At the same time, he motions for Sage to go with me. "You two go back to the house. I'll inspect the interior of my building to make sure no one has put anything inside. Magic or not, we aren't taking chances." At the sidewalk, he stops, the dog next to him. "Check the footage from last night," he tells me. "You may have caught the guy on video."

Sage brightens. "That's right. One of them is pointed over here."

She installed the motion-activated cameras, placing a spell on them to catch Trysta and any non-corporeal entities who were threatening me back in June. I kiss Logan's cheek. "You're brilliant. Be careful."

"Stay inside and don't let anyone in unless you know them."

His overprotectiveness strikes a chord in me, and I wonder if he's more aware of what's going on than I've led him to believe.

Inside the house, I lock the doors and take Sage into the kitchen. Removing Logan's plate of half eaten food, I make her sit before I pour her some coffee. "How do you like your eggs?"

Her lips move as if she's going to claim she doesn't want

anything, but she presses them together and takes a small sip of her drink. "Scrambled with onions and mushrooms."

I happen to enjoy them that way, too. I grab the ingredients from the fridge, heat the pan, and throw a couple slices of bread in the toaster slots. The urge to apologize again sits on my tongue, but I go about cooking without saying it or looking at her, giving her space to start the conversation that we need to have.

When I place the meal in front of her and hand her utensils, she stares at it for a long moment, unmoving. "I was unfair yesterday. I know you were only trying to keep me from being afraid."

I refresh my coffee and grab the toast, handing one to her and taking my seat. Spreading mine with jam, I consider my next words carefully. There's no point in sharing the results of my reading. "Water under the bridge. I'm here for you."

She digs in with gusto, and I wonder when the last time she ate was. We eat in silence for several minutes, and my mind wanders to Logan. While she finishes hers, I contact him and he immediately replies. He's fine, and his guy is on the way.

Who is this guy? I ask.

One of your favorite people. Look out the window.

Going to the front room, I gape across the street. My dad is pulling up out front.

Nash Fantome loves a good mystery, and has plenty of skills from his law days. I'm not surprised he still has the equipment to lift fingerprints.

Returning to Sage, I sit once more and bring up the app on my phone for the security cameras. "Can you think of anyone who had a reading with you that they didn't like?"

She stops mid-sip and eyes me over the brim of the cup.

"Do you think an unhappy customer is doing this? How are they making Zultan work when it's not plugged in?"

Memories flood back, this time focusing on whatever message is on the card he spit out. "I'd like to look at the interior of that machine. Maybe somebody rigged it to use batteries and a remote control."

She considers this as I review the overnight footage. "There have been two people who were upset after their readings."

"Now we're getting somewhere. Whoever it is saw Logan and Bis haul Zultan away and take it to the dump. It's clever, you have to admit, and they certainly could have replaced the original cards with their own creations to fit this scenario."

"And the snake?"

"If the cottonmouth had bit you, you could've died. It would've looked like an accident. I am highly doubtful that snake got in there on its own."

"There were no signs of a break-in."

"Are you sure all the doors and windows were locked?"

"Yes." She pauses and gets up for a refill. "Maybe it came from the cellar."

Since the building was originally a home like mine, it has a shallow one under the foundation. "Isn't there a padlock on the outside entrance?"

She nods, resuming her seat. "But I didn't check to see if it was still there."

I text Logan again. *Check the padlock on the cellar. Broken?*

While we wait for his reply, I scan the dozens of black and white clips, snapshots in time triggered by motion.

"What about Bis? Does he have any enemies who might use you to get to him?"

Her mouth drops open. "Bis? Have you met him?" She laughs. "Everyone loves him."

This is true from what I've surmised. "It's just an idea. We have to look under every stone."

In one, there's a moth close to the camera and blocking half the view of the street, in another, a cat is caught midway through the front yard, and in a third, a possum is lumbering toward the wooded lot at the end of the cul-de-sac. "Whoever returned the fortune teller didn't drive past the front of the building to drop it off, I'm afraid." Call me a dreamer, but I was hoping we had caught them in the act. Hard to get better evidence than that.

She chews a bite of toast. "The protection magic I wove into the property is strong. I don't know if they planned to put the machine inside the shop, but they must have intended harm of some kind, so it kept them from crossing the boundary."

Since the resolution of the Trysta incident, I don't keep the front cameras on during the day. I have no reason to and with the amount of people coming and going, I would have hundreds of videos to sort through. Still, I pull up those from Sunday night. With everything going on, I haven't had time to delete them. "Magic does have its uses."

She nods. "So does common sense. I need to install cameras, too, especially one pointed at the rear of the building."

"Since they drive by on the street, they must have crossed by the neighbor's yard behind you. There's an alley there. We sometimes use it when we walk to church. And that machine is heavy—it took both Logan and Bis to carry it."

"So two people are involved," she says, warming to the idea, "and somebody might have seen them lugging that thing down the alley."

Unfortunately, there's nothing there either to confirm our theory. I believe in magic and the invisible world, but knowing we have a living, breathing target—probably two— makes me feel better. Magic may be the realm of Sage and my grandmother, but tackling criminals is well within mine.

"If this person wants you dead, and they aren't above committing homicide, I can think of easier ways of carrying it out." I've had both the living, as well as a couple ghosts, try to end my life. "In my mind, even with the snake, this is intimidation. They want you out of that shop, maybe the town, but I don't believe they truly want to murder you."

"Harassment is bad enough."

"You bet your crystal ball it is." I finish my coffee and give her hand another squeeze. "And we're going to figure out who's doing it and stop them."

THIRTEEN

S age refuses to be intimidated. She insists on opening the store at ten like normal. Her sister arrives, and I'm glad to see Sage's spunk back, even though she argues vehemently that Raven should be off her feet.

On crutches, Raven isn't much help with customers, but she's an extra pair of eyes. I'm reassured that the spells on the property will keep harmful people away, but I still feel better knowing the siblings are together and Sage has someone watching her back. I promise to check on them later.

Meanwhile, Logan and I fill in my dad on what's happening. Logan found the padlock missing from the exterior cellar doors, so he asks Bis to grab one from his inventory and replace it. Bis also takes Zultan to his workshop to examine the interior.

As soon as we explain to Daddy what's transpired, he rightfully guesses this is tied to my request to run a background check on Madam X. He promises to do so as soon as possible with the limited amount of info we have. I give him the names of the two people who were upset that Sage shared with me, and he agrees to give each a call and feel them out.

While he and Logan discuss other measures to keep my friend safe, I call Rhys and quiz him about anything Madam X may have shared regarding her previous residence or employer.

"You know what I know," he tells me. "Like I said, she came from Romania and hasn't been here long."

"She's not Romanian, and I think she may be involved in threats directed towards Sage."

"What? I don't believe it. Is this why you guys tore out of The Toad last night like someone had set your backsides on fire?"

"I'm not accusing her of anything yet, so please don't mention this to her. The timing of her arrival is suspicious, and we are being overly cautious."

I can almost see him pacing his kitchen floor. "This, on top of Todd's death?" His pause is weighted and he sighs heavily. "We needed new blood, something different than what we already had to draw customers back. She seemed like the ticket."

"What do you mean *draw customers back?*"

"I didn't want to say anything, but ever since Sage opened, our psychics have seen a significant drop in clientele. Two of them couldn't afford their last booth rent and it's only fifty dollars. For a whole month! That's how bad it's been. I'm happy she's successful, but it's put a dent in our business. That, combined with this heat wave keeping people at home, has caused our bottom line to take a big hit. Now Todd's death... We're going to be in the red soon."

I'd had no idea. "I'm so sorry. Is there anything I can do?"

"Not screw up our new act. Seriously, Ava. Make sure

you have solid proof before you discredit Madam X. Even if she's eventually found innocent, you know what the gossip in this town will do to her. She's put down three months' fee for her booth. She told me she likes it here and wants to stay."

I couldn't promise anything. "Have you heard gossip at The Toad from anyone who doesn't like Sage, or might not have cared for a reading she gave them?"

He makes an exasperated noise. "From what I can tell, she's spot on every time. Yes, that upsets a few here and there. She's already got quite a reputation around here. She doesn't pull punches and she's scarily accurate."

Personally, I prefer knowing the truth of the matter, and yet, when it came to her, I only wanted to hear positive things. I can't blame some for believing they want facts, when in reality, they don't.

I end the call and return to Logan and Daddy. My father has pull with Jones since they were once partners, and the fact he recently assisted the department with a cold case. Jones owes him a favor—one like running the fingerprints Daddy has lifted off the Zultan machine through their data-bases. We already know all of ours will be on it, but since none are on file, we may have to eliminate them to single out our suspect. *Suspects*.

I share my theory about the batteries and remote control with Logan and Daddy, along with the premise that our perpetrator accessed the grounds through the rear neighbor's property. Daddy adds another thing to his list, telling me he'll drop by their place and ask if they've seen or heard anything unusual the past few nights.

Logan is already late for his meeting and drops a quick kiss on my lips before scooting off.

Reassured Sage is relatively safe, and Daddy's on the case, I clean up the kitchen and prepare for the day's workload.

A few hours later, I'm in the backyard with a client who wants a simple ceremony in my gazebo. It's her third marriage and only family for guests. She doesn't mention the weekend's events next door, which is a relief, but I keep feeling like someone is watching us. I glance across the hedge row and see Detective Jones standing in the attic window.

The humidity is less today, but the heat is still rising. Grateful for air conditioning, I offer her a glass of tea when we return inside, but she's in a hurry and asks me to email her the contract. Rosie puts her on our calendar and tells me she'll handle it. I take a break and go see how Rhys is doing.

I'm also checking as to why the detective is in their third floor window. When I slip in the back to the kitchen, no one is there, and I make it all the way upstairs without seeing a soul.

The wooden stairs leading to the top groan under my feet, but Jones doesn't turn around when I enter the space. This level is air conditioned, but a stuffy, humid cloud envelops me. I glance around at the furniture and miscellaneous boxes, shadows as heavy as the humidity.

Since he hasn't turned on any lights, the only illumination comes from the window, which he now has opened. No wonder it's warm up here.

He's studying the ledge and taking photographs with his cell.

I close the distance, not wanting to appear too nosy, but curious about what he's fascinated with. His broad shoulders block my view and I shift sideways to glance over one of them. "What are you doing?"

"What does it look like, Fantome?" he drawls.

I grit my teeth and don't correct him. I need a favor and I want to know what he's up to. "Like you're taking pictures of the window ledge."

He stares at it as if turning something over in his mind. "What are you doing here?"

"Rhys has had a difficult few days. I came to check on him, but he wasn't downstairs."

He grunts, dismissing my claim. He knows I'm here because I want to find out what he's investigating. He straightens and pockets his phone. "See these marks?"

There's a distinct line where the large window pane, now open, stripped the paint down to the bare wood. "Brax said that happened in the spring. No one had aired out the attic in a long time, and it was quite a chore to pry it open."

"Mm-hmm. That's what he told me, too. From the looks of it, I'd say someone painted this window shut a long time ago. See the ridge left on the inside?"

I do. "What about it?"

He leans forward and stares at the yard below. "You ever seen a person jump to their death?"

"Thankfully, no."

He cranks the window shut, opens it again. "If you were going to do such a thing, would you stand here"—he points to his feet on the worn wooden floor boards—"or on that ledge?"

"The ledge, I suppose. Otherwise, I'd have to jump over it."

His dark eyes slide to me and he nods. "Most jumpers don't in fact jump. They step off, fall forward. You see what I'm getting at?"

"Not exactly."

"Mr. Springer was found on his back. He was wearing thick soled shoes. Do you see any markings on this ledge that suggest he stepped onto it?"

I knew it. Not just because Todd's ghost had told me he wouldn't do such a thing, but because the detective's questions are honing in on a point. "He didn't jump."

"Well, he may have." He bends his knees slightly, mimicking the movement of jumping over the ledge. "I can't rule it out completely, but it seems if he were going to take his life, he would step onto the ledge and swan dive forward, striking the ground face first."

I shudder at the thought. "And his shoes would have left an impression in the raised paint. Could he have been pushed?"

"It does seem a possibility." He shifts sideways and acts as if he's pitching something large through the window. "Or perhaps, tossed out."

Normally, the good detective won't share details of a case with anyone, especially not me and definitely not conjecture about what might have happened. But, as long as he is... "By whom?"

He closes the window once more and locks it. "That's the question, isn't it? As far as we know, there were only four other people in the house at the time. Each of them was alone and cannot vouch for the others."

"You can't possibly think Brax or Rhys would do such a thing."

"You know what I always say about an investigation."

I wipe sweat from my brow. I'm going to need a shower after this. Setting a hand on my hip, I do my best imitation of his deep voice. "*Keep your nose out of it, Fantome.*"

He quirks a brow at me.

I try again. *"Don't go messing up my investigation, or I will arrest you for interference."*

He does a partial eye roll, as if it's too much work to do a full one. "Everyone is a suspect until they're not."

"Oh, that rule." So annoying. "They didn't even know him. What possible motive could they have? You should be looking at the Carrs."

He motions for me to keep my voice down, and I suddenly feel paranoid. I check over my shoulder to make sure nobody followed me. Jill does have a predilection for eavesdropping.

"I have no concrete evidence that this is anything other than suicide, and I need something substantial if I'm going to keep the Carrs in town."

I lower my voice. "They're staying until Wednesday."

"Perhaps." He seems unconvinced. "If, that is, I don't scare them off by asking too many follow-up questions or sniffing around them and Ms. Norwalk. I've requested an autopsy, ruling it as a suspicious death, and since Mr. Springer has no relatives, she's hanging around until he's released."

"She didn't mention that when I spoke to her earlier."

"She's had quite a shock. Doesn't seem to know what to think."

It dawns on me why he's sharing all of this. "You want me to ask your questions and see what I can dig up."

"Makes sense that you would be over here frequently, checking on your friends." He studies an antique lamp to my left. "And you did claim that Mr. Springer's ghost insisted he didn't jump. Why don't you ask him to tell you what *did* happen, and point me in the direction of our killer? If there is one," he adds.

"Todd's spirit hasn't been around again. What exactly do you want me to ask the Carrs about? And why would you be sniffing around Todd's fiancée? Sandra wasn't even here when it occurred."

He tips his chin down in what might pass for a nod, but it's clear he has doubts. "So everyone claims, but she is the only one out of all of our potential suspects who actually knew him."

Huh. Could Sandra have snuck into the house and done this without anyone seeing her? "I know the spouse or partner is the first one you look at when its homicide, but her? Really? She seems totally distraught, and they were about to get married. What's the motive?"

He steps away from the window, out of the sunlight coming through it. "You think like your daddy. What you must remember is, motive is similar to that windowsill"—he points to it—"sometimes you have to scratch off some paint to reveal it."

Jones has turned philosophical on me. "Do you want me to buddy up to her and find out with their relationship was like?"

"Every couple has their problems."

While that might be true, my gut says Sandra is no killer. "Have you asked any of them about the note Todd left? Do you think it was forged?"

"The handwriting appears to match his name in the register, but that's a small sampling. I've requested Ms. Norwalk submit something more in-depth that I can compare it to, but she claims not to have anything like that. Mr. Springer apparently didn't keep any kind of journal or notebook, using email and text for correspondence."

"Welcome to the 21st Century." I glance at the doorway

again. "She doesn't even have a love letter from him? A note of any kind?"

Jones shakes his head. "Seems he was not overly demonstrative in showing affection."

"I overheard Gordon say Sandra doesn't believe the note."

"Oh?" It's not often he shows surprise. "She said nothing of that nature to me."

I think about it for a minute, considering what he wants me to do. We've worked together before and it nearly got me killed. "If I do this, I want something in return."

His face is expressionless. "Such as?"

"Sage is being harassed by an unknown party. They're making threats against her life."

"Nash told me. What do you want me to do? You have no suspect, not even a person of interest at this point."

"I do, too. Madam X."

"You don't even know her real name, or where she's from. That's not enough to rule her out, but like with Mr. Springer's death, motive seems to be the missing key."

I don't disagree. "All I'm asking is that you help Daddy any way you can to find out who's behind the threats. I'm taking this seriously, and I'll send you anything I come up with, but I want you to take it seriously, as well."

He reaches into his breast pocket and brings out a folded slip of paper. "A list of questions I'd like answers to."

"Does this mean we have a deal?"

He strolls for the door and the stairs leading down. "We do, Fantome. Now get to work."

FOURTEEN

y first order of business is to talk to Todd, I just have to figure out how. I head across the street to Tea Leaves and wait until Sage is free of customers.

In the workroom, I tell her and Raven what I want. "I need to hold a séance and speak to Todd Springer's ghost. There's lingering suspicion around his death and I need to know everything he remembers, even if he doesn't know who pushed, tossed, or threw him out that window."

Neither sister seems surprised. "Tonight?" Sage asks.

"If you're free. Seven-ish?"

They nod in unison, and it's the first time I notice how strong their family resemblance is.

"Also, you know how you get sick and you do a search on Web MD for your symptoms, and the next thing you know, you're convinced you're dying in three days from some rare disease?"

They stare at me, seemingly puzzled. I continue. "What?" Sage asks.

"What I'm getting at is that you need a second opinion. Even if I were to see a medical doctor for an illness, and he or she told me I needed surgery or some kind of treatment, it's always wise to check with another professional and get the diagnosis confirmed."

Sage toys with her earring. "What are you getting at?"

"I don't care for Madam X, and as much as it grieves me to say this, her reading may have been correct. I want you to get a second opinion though, and I want you to get it from my friend, Winter."

The sisters exchange a glance. "That's a good idea," Raven says.

Sage narrows her eyes. "Is she going to be all puppy dogs and rainbows because she knows I'm your friend? Or will she tell me the truth?"

"She always tells the truth."

"I like her already. She's the one who sees ghost, too, isn't she?"

I take out my phone. "I'll text you her number. You can set up a call or a video chat. It will give us all perspective, and maybe reveal an avenue we need to pursue."

An hour later at my place, I'm turning over ideas about how to work Jones' questions into conversation with the Carrs and Sandra. In fact, how to start a conversation about Todd in the first place, without sounding nosy, rude, or just plain crazy. I don't advertise my mediumship, but I consider telling them individually that he's spoken to me and pointed a finger at them. Their reactions might be worth it.

When something is vexing me, I often doodle. With my upcoming honeymoon, I've been sketching a trousseau, including the lingerie. Gloria is eager to build it for me.

Another potential line to include with my bridal gowns. My imagination never stops.

While speaking to a client on the phone, I've drawn a series of panties and matching bras. Bis bursts in, hearing me from the entryway and rushing to my office with a bag in hand. "Look what I found!"

I hold up a finger, and he makes a face, seeing I'm busy. *Sorry*, he mouths. His attention drops to the sketchpad, he blushes, whirls, and takes several giant steps back out to the foyer.

Rosie greets him and asks if she can help him with anything. He shakes his head.

I wrap up my call and put the drawings away. "Hey, Bis. What did you find?"

He returns, dumping out a handful of miscellaneous gadgets onto my desk. His eyes don't meet mine, and I smile because he's blushing again. "I took that bloody thing apart and this is what I found."

I study what looks to be wires and electronic parts. "Inside the Zultan machine? What is all that?"

He picks up a small round cylinder with a lens. "This is a camera with a motion detector, similar to your security ones. It was embedded on the metal piece where the cards come out." He sets that down and lifts what looks like a speaker attached to some wires. "This baby was piggybacked onto the mannequin's voice box, and is controlled by a remote. And this"—he switches out the speaker for a square box—"is a Wi-Fi connecter."

I can make a good guess as to what the menagerie suggests, but I'm less than an expert at technology. "None of this is normal for the interior workings of that machine?"

He walks me through it. "The motion detector triggers

the camera and whoever is on the other end knows who's standing there, thanks to the Wi-Fi. They could then use the remote control on their end to speak to you and control the mannequin's actions."

Bingo. "I thought as much. I had Sherlock examine the interior for spirits, but he wouldn't know a Wi-Fi router from a cat. They weren't using magic, and our fortune teller is not a legitimate divination tool. Someone's been yanking our chains."

"Exactly. They didn't need to be nearby to see Logan and I haul it from the shop and to the dump. The camera kicked in as soon as we got near it, and would've showed them the view on the drive there." He punches the top of the desk lightly. "But, they're not as smart as they think. RIP Zultan. He won't be showing them anything now, or freaking out my girlfriend."

I smile and sit back in my chair, relieved. "Whoever did this went to a lot of trouble to spook her." And the rest of us in the process. "Have you told her about this?"

"She's pissed. I wouldn't want to be them when she discovers who they are. She's going to hex them to Hades and back."

And I was going to cheer her on when she did it. "That antiques dealer she bought this from? Could he be behind something like this?"

The front door opens and Sage storms in, hearing my question. "I've known Leo Kingsley since I was a girl. There's no way."

"Then how did the person know you would end up with that machine? How would they rig it with all this stuff?"

"I've been racking my brain, and I think I know."

"They broke the cellar lock and put a snake in the shop," Bis offers. "They could have rewired Zultan then."

"Possibly, but it's more likely the handyman I hired to fix it." She points to the mess on my desk. "When I got the machine, it was glitchy. I would plug it in, turn him on, and he would sputter. His eyes would flicker and go out. His voice would cut out in the middle of a word and then come back. I figured there was a short in the wiring and I felt super lucky to find a guy who had worked on them before."

"Why didn't you ask me to take a look at it?" Bis inquired.

"In all your spare time? You've been so busy, I've barely seen you, and besides, electrical work isn't your favorite. I didn't want to bother you with this."

He leans over and gives her a quick peck on the cheek. "Who is this guy?"

"LaCosta Hoyt. He came by the day Leo's delivery guys brought Zultan over. The thing was sitting in my front room initially, because I had planned to have it on display as a game for kids and stuff. While he was in the shop, he said he had experience with them and left me his business card, in case it needed maintenance. It was right after that when it started acting up."

"So you hired him to fix it?" I clarify.

She nods. "We set it in the back, and after he initially inspected it, he said he had to order some parts. He returned last week and installed them, but, as you all saw, it continued to be glitchy."

"I'd call that more than a glitch. We need to talk to this Hoyt fellow."

"I already dialed his number. The phone isn't active anymore."

I do a quick online search. "There's no one by that name in the local area, and I've never heard of him. The only thing that comes up is a gaming avatar." I squint at the screen. "He's a wizard, apparently. In some Morcar Magic game...?"

Neither of them have heard of it.

"Should I gather this stuff," Bis asks, pointing to the gadgets, "and take it to your dad? Maybe he can track the guy down."

"Leave it with me. I'll have Jones look into it."

Sage gives me a skeptical snort. "He won't do anything. He hates me."

"Hate is a strong word, but he's not my biggest fan either. It doesn't stop him from upholding the law and protecting those he serves. Trust me, he owes me a favor, and he'll check into it."

Sage goes on her toes and kisses Bis. "I got to get back. Thank you."

It's good to see her fired up again. Before she walks out the door, she turns and says to me, "Thank you, too."

I hold up a hand by way of acceptance, and she's gone.

"I better do the same," Bis says. "Dad's ready to string me up for taking time off for this."

I shoo him toward the exit. "Great job. I'm holding a séance tonight, by the way, in case you want to attend."

He brightens. "What time?"

"Seven."

"Did Lia talk you into it?"

Gah, I haven't checked in with her. "No, I'm not inviting her to this."

He shrugs. "Too bad. I bet she'd love it. Who are you summoning?"

"Todd Springer."

"The jumper?"

"The one and only."

He rubs his hands together in anticipation. "I'll be here."

After he's gone, Rosie meanders in. "It seems I've missed a lot."

I pull out the sketchpad and fill her in, doodling once more. She sits and listens, fascinated with my rambling stories. "How are you going to question them?" She hooks a thumb over her shoulder toward the B&B.

RIP Zultan, I write in the margin of my notepad. "I'm not sure... Wait!" I snap my fingers and silently thank Bis for the inspiration. Shoving the pad back in my top drawer, I shoot to my feet. "I have to talk to Rhys. Can you handle our two o'clock?"

She glances at her watch. "Of course. I know that look. Go. Do whatever you have to do."

Rushing to her side, I lean over and hug her. "Thank you."

"Sounds like you have plenty for tonight's séance, but if you need another warm body, I'm available."

"You're the best," I call as I head for the back door.

"I know," she replies.

Over at the B&B, I catch Rhys in the backyard, weeding a flower bed. "Hey," I say. "I have an idea."

He sits on his heels and shucks off his gardening gloves before wiping his face on his shirt sleeve. "For what?"

"It's a way to honor Todd and find some closure."

He gives me a perplexed look. "Um...okay."

"It was a shocking event. All of you are traumatized by it, and poor Todd has no relatives. No one to grieve for him, outside of Sandra. That's a lot for her to handle all on her own. She's in shock."

"We all are," he agrees, coming to his feet and wiping at the grass stains on his knees.

"Exactly. You need peace about this affair."

The corners of his eyes narrow, suspicious. "What's your idea?"

"Let's honor him and his life. We'll hold a memorial service."

A slow smile spreads over his face. "I like it. When should we do it? Tonight?"

"Does five work? That will give us enough natural light, but my backyard will be shaded."

He flaps his hands in the air. "Heavens! I have a ton to do to pull it off!"

"I'll handle it. Events are what I do, after all."

"It's a wonderful suggestion." He hugs me, leaving a smattering of soil on my blouse. "There must be something I can help with."

"Supply the booze, and lots of it."

His expression turns wary once more and he studies me. "What are you up to, Ava Fantome-Cross?"

I affect an expression of pure innocence, much like I used to when Mama caught me reading after bedtime. "Just make sure the Carrs and Sandra attend, okay? Be at the gazebo at five. See you then."

FIFTEEN

W hen Jenn arrives, I put her on decoration duty, placing an altar we use for weddings inside the center of the gazebo with candles on it. I wish I had a photo of Todd to place there, too, but since I don't, this will have to do for a focal point.

I call Betty and ask her deliver a wreath and then I alert all those I can recruit to join us. Reverend Stout is delighted when I request he say a few words. I consider telling Jones my plan, but I don't want him to crash the party. That will put everyone on edge and keep lips closed.

After several hours stewing about it, I send Lia a text, inviting her to the service, as well. A detective is only as good as her eyes, ears, and wits. Tonight, everyone from my parents, Sage, and Bis, to Lia, will be mine to ferret out our killer. It's a long shot, but I coach each of them to sniff around, listen to conversations, and report back anything they hear.

Jenn and Rosie are curious and both offer to stay, but I send them home. They have families to care for and I don't want to overwhelm Sandra and the Carrs. Too many strangers could backfire.

They do help me set up the music and speakers, arrange the wreath and light the candles. Jenn has set up our white chairs by the time Queenie arrives with plates of finger foods.

While music plays and Sandra weeps in one of the seats, I welcome Jill and Gordon. Jill checks out the decor and nods approvingly, while Gordon looks like he might be sick.

The weather is sticky but there's a breeze and the fairy lights twinkle. Tabby appears in cat form, and Samuel hovers around, eagle-eyed.

Neither Persephone nor Sherlock show. I send my guardian angel a mental message to at least attend the séance later.

Reverend Stout gives a lovely, if generic, eulogy. Sandra adds a few words, making Todd sound like the best guy ever. It's touching and everyone acts properly sad over his passing. Mama leads us in a chorus of *Amazing Grace*, and the reverend closes things with a prayer.

Afterwards, Brax and Rhys hand out wine in plastic cups and Queenie passes her food trays around. Daddy pulls me aside. "I've got nothing on your psychic."

"There's a bag of electronics on my desk. Bis found a system inside the Zultan machine that someone was using to harass Sage. Could be our Madam X. Can you take it to Jones for me? Meanwhile, do you know a guy named LaCosta Hoyt?"

"Never heard of him."

"He's the next person I need you to investigate. Like Madam X, I believe he's using an alias, but he's most likely the person who put the electronics inside the carnival game. They may be working together."

He raises his red plastic cup. "I'm on it."

I mosey over to Jill, who is selecting a sandwich. "I heard you play the piano."

She nods, taking a bite. "Learned from my grandmother." A wave of her hand encompasses the yard. "This is nice. Especially on such short notice."

Queenie encourages us to take another miniature sandwich. "Try the ham and watercress."

Jill does, while I pass. "It would be lovely if you played something at your grandmother's birthday party."

Queenie's eyes light up. "I bet she would love it! That would be the perfect gift!"

Jill swallows and shakes her head. "Trust me, it wouldn't. She was a professional. A famous jazz artist back in the day. Me? I'm terrible."

"Famous? Do I know her?"

Reverend Stout calls to Queenie, asking if she has more egg salad and she excuses herself, but not before she says, "You've heard of her, Ava. Teresa Bird. She played once at the speakeasy." A wink and she's gone.

"The Cross barn?" I'm flummoxed. "How perfect to hold her party there, then."

Jill chugs some wine. "I knew she grew up around here, but I didn't know there even was a speakeasy."

I fill her in about it as we stroll toward the homestead. "I'll make sure there's a piano—a properly tuned one—in case either of you wants to tickle the ivories."

Jill waves a hand. "She can't. Her arthritis is too bad and she can't see anymore. It's a shame, she hasn't been the same since she had to stop."

"My dad is a musician. Semi-famous, even. He was in a band, but then went solo."

"That's nice." She seems bored. "Grams was in bands in her heyday, but she could sing and went off on her own for twenty years." She pulls out her phone and shows me a sepia-toned photo. "That's her before she met my grandfather."

We stop at the creek, deep in shadows. The crickets and locusts are revving up. I study the picture but don't detect even the slightest resemblance. "She's beautiful. Did they have a big family?"

"Only my dad." She puts the phone away and finishes her wine. "Neither of us got her genes, I'm afraid. Dad was tone deaf and I don't have the dexterity with the keyboard she had."

Persephone appears out of nowhere and I startle. "Ask her about her father."

"Does your dad live around here?"

"He passed a few weeks ago."

"I'm so sorry."

"Don't be." She studies the farmhouse. "He was never around. Disappointed me, Mom, and Grams. I think that's why she and Grams bonded. She needed someone to fill the hole my dad left. Plus, I was his only child, and her only grandchild. She probably worried that Mom would take off with me if she upset her."

I have no idea why this is important and give Persephone a questioning glance while Jill eyes the creek. "Ask about the portfolio," my guardian angel instructs.

As if that's not a weird, random question. "Does your grandmother have a portfolio of songs?"

Jill smiles. "Huge. And it's apparently in demand. Who

knew? She's living meagerly, when that thing is worth millions."

"Really?"

"She worked with three of the big singers back then, and has a bunch of off-the-cuff jam sessions she recorded in secret. That, combined with her enormous collection, was recently appraised at three million. Meanwhile, she stays in a rundown duplex and tries to mop her own floors. Ridiculous."

She strolls toward the crowd, Gordon on his fourth or fifth glass of wine. I follow, still not understanding why any of this is important. "That's a lot of money."

"I've finally convinced her to auction off the whole thing." We end up back in the main yard, and she pauses for Rhys to refill her cup. "It's not doing any of us any good, and we could use those funds."

"Sounds like a good idea." I notice Lia waving me over. Persephone is gone again. "Will you excuse me?"

I meet up with the teenager, who is shoving down sandwiches as fast as she can swallow. She beams. "These are fantastic. Hey, I'm sorry I lost it the other day over that stupid Zultan machine. Sage told me what's going on. Have you seen Todd's ghost yet?"

"Keep your voice down, please." I glance around but the various groups aren't paying attention to us. "He hasn't appeared, and I'm glad you're feeling better."

"Rude, don't you think?"

"I wasn't trying to be."

"No, no." She swallows another sandwich. "Not you. Todd. We're having a memorial for him and he doesn't even show? Jeez."

"Ghosts can be that way," I say, eyeing Sandra, who is

downing a shot of whiskey, courtesy of my husband. "Unreliable and often absent when you want to talk to them."

"Are we going back to see Avenger?"

"Maybe," I tell her. "Have you seen or heard anything suspicious from our guests?"

"Sandra's been flirting with Logan, that's about it. Oh, and she said something like Todd would hate the music. He didn't care for gospel or instrumental. Hey, maybe that's why he stayed away."

Truth was, I'd believe it. "Thanks." I have another idea brewing. I catch up with Sandra and smile at Logan. "Sandra, I hope you enjoyed our impromptu service. I know it wasn't much, but we're family around here and felt we needed to memorialize him in some small way."

She's on the verge of being drunk. I decide to forgive her for chatting up my husband, even though she's supposed to be in mourning and he's not on the market. This may, in fact, be her way of suppressing her grief. "Lovely," she says a bit tipsy. "Hot, but lovely."

"Lia mentioned you were unhappy with the music selection. I apologize for not asking you about Todd's preferences."

"His tastes weren't exactly great either. Lately, it was all jazz." She makes a face. "Awful stuff."

Gordon and Jill are a few yards away, Mama keeping them occupied. I remind myself to hug her extra hard tonight. "Modern jazz or the older variety?"

"That old swing stuff." She sniffs. "Never cared for any of it myself."

"Was he a fan of Teresa Bird?"

She shrugs and sips. "Could be. He bought a bunch of vintage LPs, if you can believe it, about a month ago. Had to buy an old player, too. Listened to them nonstop. Drove me crazy. We had a fight about it right before..." Her face falls and tears shine in her eyes. "I'm such a fool. I should have been more considerate. He had no family, only me, and I should have..." She breaks out balling and rushes off to the B&B.

Logan glances at me. "What was that about?"

"Not sure, but I've got a feeling."

He winks. "I figured. You have that look on your face."

"What look?"

He grins and kisses my forehead. "You get a cute little crease right between your eyebrows." He raises the bottle. "Need a drink?"

"Better keep my head clear."

Jill is staring at us, alerted by Sandra's crying. "Is she okay?"

"I'll go check on her," Rhys volunteers.

"Thanks," I say, then to Jill, "She just needs a minute."

Reverend Stout hails me. "Thank you for holding this service for our brother."

"I know it was last minute, but I appreciate you leading it."

"Happy to do so. I hadn't realized he was the baby that was left on our steps thirty years ago."

"The *what*?"

He nods and points to his cheek. "Sandra showed me a picture. Todd had a teardrop birthmark on his cheek, just like that baby."

I'm flummoxed. "I had no idea there had ever been a child left on your steps." I also didn't realize he'd been preaching that long. On one hand, he seems to have been here forever, but on the other, he must've been a young man when he took over the parish. "Who was the mother?"

"No idea. My wife wanted to keep the boy, but Children's Services had a long list of people wanting a healthy male baby already. Broke her heart." He smiles. "God moves in mysterious ways, and we must trust in his guidance. He knew what was best for Todd. I'm just sorry he didn't come and see me before he decided to end his life."

My mind whirls. "Do you think the mother was someone local? What about the father?"

"Never learned their identities. Either could've been sitting in Sunday services every week, and I wouldn't have known they were the child's parents. It's possible the mother came from a different town to be sure her identity was kept secret, yet I always had a feeling it was somebody local. The gossip mill claimed he belonged to the Coperites, but I never believed it."

"Coperites?"

"They had no home. Drove around in a tiny car, and the children never went to school."

"That sort of rings a bell. I was under the impression that was a local legend."

"We extended a hand to them multiple times, but were always refused. They were loners, and seemed to always be on the run from someone—the police, Child Services, you get the idea."

"But you didn't think the boy was theirs?"

"When we found him on the steps, he was clean, didn't smell, and he was wrapped in a brand new blanket with a toy beside him. I'll always remember that. It was a parakeet, bold, primary colors. He loved that thing, nearly as big as he was.

When I told Sandra about it, she claimed Todd still had it. At first, she thought it was ridiculous that a grown man kept a dirty, old, stuffed animal, but when he explained it was the only link he had to his mother, she realized why it was important to him."

"He was adopted, then?"

"He was. Sandra said they were killed in a car accident five years ago. That's when he started searching for his birth mother. It's tough on a man when he doesn't have family. Sandra said he wanted to have lots of kids, but I got the impression she wasn't keen on that."

The reverend touches my arm and says goodbye. "Please tell her she's welcome to leave her car at the church parking lot as long as she needs to."

"Before you go, you haven't noticed any unusual activity, have you? Like people carrying things down the alley behind Sage's shop?"

"Can't say I have, but since they rented out Perry Buchanan's house down the block from us, there's been a host of people coming and going from that place. I know it's wrong to jump to conclusions, but I hope we don't have drugs or something else going on there."

"Have you talked to Detective Jones about it?"

Jill is suddenly by my side. Stout shakes his head. "It's probably nothing," he says. "I better run."

"Have they gotten the autopsy results, yet?" Jill asks as he walks away.

"Not that I've heard. Why?"

She shrugs, but there's tension in her shoulders. "I didn't realize they were doing one. Your father just told me. What in the world would they need that for?"

"I'm sure it's a precaution. You'll have to ask Detective Jones."

"No wonder Sandra's so upset. Can you imagine? It's bad enough that her fiancé killed himself, and now they're cutting him open to try and find out if he was murdered?"

While that is oftentimes why they perform an autopsy, it's curious to me that her mind went there. I consider Jones' questions. "I suppose because it's a suspicious death, the police are simply covering all the bases. We must be sure."

"Suspicious? The man left a note. What is there to be suspicious about?"

Perfect opening. "He was alone, and no one can validate that they saw him jump of his own volition."

She laughs, the sound brittle in the air, and waves her cup around, sloshing wine over the side. It barely misses my foot and I step back. "Oh, that's ridiculous. They want money, plain and simple. Find a way to sucker the bereaved and insurance company out of some cash."

I don't comment, keeping my face neutral.

She takes my silence for an invitation to continue. The cup stops swinging and her eyes light up. "You know what? Now that I think about it, I remember hearing voices when I was in the tub enjoying my bath. They were far away and the woman's sounded rather whiney. At the time, I thought Todd had his TV on, or maybe he was on speakerphone, but it sounded like they were in the attic." She stares across the lawn to the B&B and focuses on the upper window.

"Did you tell Jones this?"

She doesn't answer, but turns wide eyes on me, as if a thought has just occurred. "Do you think Sandra was actually here already and they were in the attic arguing?"

I let the idea sink in. It's not out of reason. She's been parking at the church—what if she arrived before anyone but

Todd knew? Was there more to her and Todd's argument over the music? Did his past as an orphan play into it?

"Would you excuse me?" I ask the woman. "I need to go grab some fresh ice tea."

I don't wait for her to respond and head inside. I may not have gotten answers to all of his questions, but I may have landed even more. It's time to call Jones.

SIXTEEN

The detective doesn't say much when I tell him all I've learned. I don't even get a "good job" or any speculation on his part if Sandra, or Jill and Gordon for that matter, are connected to Todd's demise.

The memorial ends while I'm writing notes to myself, trying to puzzle out the links, my team of spies drifting in and gathering in the kitchen.

Taking my notepad with me, I join them and we share information. Mama and Queenie remember when the Stouts found the child on the church steps, but he was only a few weeks old at the time and the state took him away before most folks even saw him.

"Do you really think he was murdered?" Mama asks me. "That poor man."

"And in my son's place!" Queenie isn't one to swear, but I can tell she wants to. "I will string up whoever did it!"

"Mom," Brax says, patting her arm, "if it was homicide, which we don't know for sure yet, we'll let the police deal with it."

"Don't you 'mom' me," she retorts, fire in her eyes. "No one messes with my boys and gets away from the wrath of Queenie LaFleur!" She grabs both Brax and Rhys and hugs them.

The two accept her embrace, Brax rolling his eyes at me over her shoulder.

"I saw that, young man," she says, and we all laugh.

"Eyes in the back of her head," Mama states.

"Just like you." I throw an arm around her.

"I'm not going to need dinner tonight after all that good food," Bis says to Queenie. Then to me, he adds, "Anytime you want to use me for undercover work, feed me Queenie's sandwiches, and I'll be at your service."

"Noted." I glance at the group. "Thank you all for coming. I'll keep you posted on further developments."

"We should set up for the séance," Sage says. She tugs Bis with her. "I'll grab my stuff and get Raven."

Lia, sitting on the kitchen counter, perks up like someone has offered her a million dollars. "A séance? You didn't tell me we were doing one of those tonight."

"You're not—" Too late, she's already off and dashing after Sage.

"Ava," Mama starts, "I don't think it's healthy for that young girl to be involved in...you know, *ghost stuff*."

I couldn't agree more. "Don't worry," I tell her. I guide her and Daddy to the front door. "I'll handle it."

Once I've got them on their way, Brax and Rhys ask if there's anything else they need to do. "If one of them is a murderer," Rhys states, "are we safe?"

It's a reasonable concern. "I think so, and if Detective Jones felt you were in danger, I'm sure he would say so. All the same, keep your wits about you. "

Brax pats his back, and his mother steps to the other side of Rhys, linking her arm with his. "They touch one hair on your heads, and I'll make them pay."

Rhys smiles, but it's weak. "I know you will, Miss Queenie."

With a glance at me, she marches them to the back, looking as fierce as I've ever seen her. "You watch yourself, Avalon," she says. "With the living and the dead."

"Yes, ma'am."

Logan rubs my shoulders, the tension coiled in them slowly easing. "That was a great idea about the service. You learned a lot."

Sage and Bis return with Raven and the sisters place a black cloth over the kitchen table.

"It's all tied together somehow," I tell Logan, watching Sage pull out candles and a smudge bundle.

He and I get extra chairs and line them up, but before we can join the others, the doorbell rings. Logan and I exchange a look, then he accompanies me to see who it is.

I open the door to find two unexpected—unwanted—visitors. "What are you doing here?"

On the porch stands Jones. As if things couldn't get any weirder, next to him is Madam X. "She says you're doing a séance to speak to my deceased victim," Jones draws. "You didn't think to invite me?"

"How did you know..." I stare at the woman. "Did you bug my house, too?"

She brushes past me and moves around Logan. "I have nothing to do with that carnival game, and you need my help."

Walking through the place like she's been here before,

she disappears into the kitchen. Instantly, I hear Sage and Bis arguing with her.

"Play along," Jones says under his breath to us. "Maybe we'll catch two criminals tonight."

He, too, brushes past, gathering with the others and raising his voice to stop the argument. Dumbfounded, I stand there with the door open staring at Logan. He shakes his head and shrugs.

"We gonna do this?" Jones yells to us. "I don't have all night."

"Want me to throw him out?" Logan asks.

Yes. "Not yet. If he wants to stay for this, so be it."

"And Madam X?"

I grit my teeth. "I don't like it, but maybe she'll show her hand."

We fist bump and then reconvene in the kitchen.

We have to pull the table farther from the wall and crowd in. When I again attempt to send Lia home, she shows me a text from her mother, giving her permission to stay. "I told her everything," the girl retorts. "She's totally cool with it. She even asked if she could come." She points to a follow-up message.

I wouldn't be surprised if the woman did. "We don't have any more room at the inn," I say.

Lia makes a face. "Huh?"

"Never mind."

Sage lights the candles, sending scowls to the psychic. Lia rubs her hands together in anticipation, and Logan decides to stay out of the circle, leaning against the countertop behind me. Sage sits and instructs us to hold hands. "Ready?" she asks me.

As I'll ever be. I have Madam X and Lia on either side of

me. I place my hands palm up on the table and each of them takes one. "Ready."

Sage tells us to close our eyes while she recites her opening invocation, asking our spirit guides to protect us and open the door to the afterlife. She adds a few words to extend the sight to the group, as long as they maintain contact, and I realize my grandmother has taught her another new spell.

I peek at the participants and find Jones watching me. For a split second, I think about sticking my tongue out at him, but I stop myself. I'm an adult. I need to act like it.

Persephone and Sherlock hover, literally, in the doorway. I raise a questioning brow to her, mentally asking if there's something she wants me to know, and her focus trails to the woman next to me.

A pregnant silence has fallen, and I realize Sage is waiting for me to reach out to Todd's spirit. I clear my throat and glance at my notepad, where I have written a series of questions I want to ask him. "Todd Springer, I call you to this circle to speak to us."

Not as eloquent as Sage's words, but it should do the job.

Nothing happens, and everyone opens their eyes, peering around. They land on me, expecting me to do something else.

Ghosts frustrate me, and tonight, I'm already on edge with everything going on next door, as well as the fact Madam X is sitting next to me holding my hand. I feel like I'm sleeping with the enemy, and I swear I will get Jones back for this. "Come on, Todd. This is your chance to tell us what happened. I held a memorial service for you. The least you can do is talk to me."

Nothing.

"I'm not going to sit here all night begging. Enter the circle now."

"Is this how you normally speak to the dead?" Madam X asks, seemingly affronted.

"I'm sure you're more professional at this than I am," I say with heavy sarcasm, "but yes. I've found the direct approach works best."

Sage snickers. Logan touches my back in solidarity. The corner of Jones' mouth quirks. Lia simply nods enthusiastically. "Ava knows what she's doing. You might learn something from her."

Madam X rears back. "You, child, should watch your manners."

I squeeze the woman's hand hard. "You busted into my house without invitation and included yourself in this séance. Let me be direct with you, as well. Leave the girl alone. She's an esteemed guest; you are *not*."

Persephone grins and Sherlock gives me a thumbs-up. Lia beams, giving the woman a smug smile.

"Who is the ghost in the doorway?" Madam X asks.

Sherlock lowers his hand. Those with their backs to the doorway turn to look at it.

"That's Sherlock," Bis informs her.

Jones doesn't know he's a medium, too, and raises a brow.

I study the psychic. "He's a friend, not our Mr. Springer."

She huffs. "Making friends with ghosts is dangerous."

"You let me worry about that."

The lights flicker, as does the candle, and Lia says, "Um, Ava?"

Tabby is in her lap when I glance over. The cat's eyes are

focused on the center candle, the flame growing exponentially as we all gawk.

It has taken shape, and both Jones and Lia shove their chairs back, their hands falling apart.

Sage yells, "Don't break the circle!"

They clasp hands once more. The flame grows and becomes the upper torso of a man.

This is new.

He glances around, spinning in the air until he finds me. "I didn't jump," Todd Springer declares, "but I don't know who killed me."

Regaining my composure, I try to appear friendly. I reel off the second question on my list, since he obviously can't answer the first and most important. "Who wrote the suicide note?"

"Suicide note? That was a breakup letter to Sandra. I realized we weren't compatible and I was about to reunite with my birth family. I wanted a fresh start, and she..."

Jones leans forward. "She what?"

Todd whirls to face him, then once more turns to me. "I needed that connection—to my birth dad. I hired a private detective to find him, or my mom, and I learned that she was dead, but that he was still alive. I was scared, but I reached out to him and asked him to meet. He agreed to it, but when I showed up, he didn't. I thought he'd rejected me. A few weeks later, I learned he had died." He hangs his head, and I feel a wave of sadness ripple out from him. He chuckles without humor. "What are the odds? I didn't even get to meet him face-to-face. I didn't know what to do. I found his obituary, saw that I had other relatives. I was torn between contacting them, or just giving up. I'd lived thirty years without them, but was it fair to any of us for me to barge into their lives?"

"I'm so sorry." I can't imagine what it must've been like for him. I want to hug my parents all over again. "What did you do?"

"I took the biggest risk of my life—I contacted the woman I believed was my sister. Explained what had happened. I asked if we could at least talk." He shakes his head, another wave of sadness flooding out of him. "She said I was a con man, told me there was no way I was her brother, and she knew I was after the family money. I didn't even know there was any. I wanted to prove to them that I was telling the truth. I asked about doing a DNA test, but she threatened me. Told me never to contact them again."

"Not cool," Lia says. "I think it would be awesome to find a long lost brother!"

He gives her a weak smile. "I got a test anyway, and I made her an offer—to meet me, see I was telling the truth, and I told her I would be willing to sign any kind of statement or contract, declaring I wasn't interested in any family money or inheritance."

"Did she take you up on it?" I ask.

He shakes his head. "Not at first, so I told her I would reach out to another member of the family. I wasn't giving up. That did the trick. All of a sudden, she was willing to connect. Told me to be sure to bring my results. Something told me her change of heart was suspicious." He stares at a spot on the far wall. "I wanted to trust her, wanted to trust them all, whoever was left. I dreamed of a reunion, Christmases, birthday parties, you know? That's all I wanted. Not their money."

"Did you meet her?" Jones asks.

"She planned to meet me here in Thornhollow, but I ended up dead. I can't remember exactly what happened, why I was in that window. I kept feeling drawn to that old piano, though. Weird, right?"

The piano. The sister. The dead father. "You were meeting Jill Carr?"

His form flickers. "I feel sick."

"Answer the question," Jones demands.

"I can't"—he flickers again and his body twists—"hold *oonnn*."

Madam X looks frantic. "Do something! He's fading!"

With a pop, Todd vanishes and the flame shrinks to normal. Sighs echo in the room, some with relief, others with frustration. "Todd," I command. "Return to the circle. Please."

Nothing happens except the candle's shadow dancing on the walls. Madam X snorts. "I can see the direct approach works well. You should be more respectful of the dead and they will be more apt to cooperate."

Okay, maybe she does see ghosts. Big deal. That doesn't mean she's accurate with predictions. "You should be more respectful of your host," I say with fake charm. "Seems to me, you have a lot to answer for. Perhaps we should be interrogating you, instead of that poor soul."

"Fantome," Jones warns.

I pin him with the glare. "Fantome-Cross!"

Logan strokes my shoulders again. "Everybody take a deep breath. What do we do now?"

"Don't break the circle," Persephone says quietly.

Madam X starts to pull away, as do the others. "Wait another minute," I tell them, although hanging onto this woman's hand is the last thing I want to do. "Todd Springer, return to us."

The candle flame bursts upward, once, twice, three times. Each grows bigger, but the flame is wild, the red and orange colors gyrating back-and-forth, side to side. Instinctively, we all tip backwards from it, even as we hold the circle once more.

"You can do it, Todd," I coach. "We want to help you, and make sure whoever did this to you pays. But we need answers."

Leaping again, the flame once more becomes the upper body of a man.

It's not Todd.

Avenger, the spirit from the morgue, dives at my face. "Hey there, ghost hunter. Remember me?"

A squeak erupts from my mouth and I jump, but I don't let go of Madam X or Lia. I'm about to be consumed by the candle flame when the psychic raises our combined hands and surprises me once again by punching Avenger in the nose.

Our hands go through him, but it seems to startle him enough that he jerks. "Who are you?" Madam X asks. "We didn't call you."

"I am Avenger!" He says it with such gusto, I almost expect him to beat his chest. "I've been desecrated. I demand justice! An eye for an eye."

Lia's eyes are as big as saucers. "It's really him! Hey, I'm the ghost hunter, by the way. Not Ava. She's just a medium."

Just. While it's not Todd, maybe I can get answers for Dr. Earnestine. "Desecrated, how?"

"He cut me up." Fiery fingers point to different parts of his torso. "He took my organs."

"Who did? Dr. Latimer, the morgue physician?"

"How dare he! He had no right!"

"He had to perform an autopsy. That's what they do. They cut you open and check out your organs."

He shakes his head vehemently. "That was no autopsy. They pulled the plug. They *let me die.*" His voice breaks on the last word. He rallies. "I will have my vengeance!"

He sweeps, diving at me again. This time, it's Lia who stops him. Jumping to her feet, Tabby scattering, the girl leans forward and blows out the candle.

SEVENTEEN

My protégé is shaken, and I feel bad about what happened. I shouldn't have allowed her to attend this, even if she had permission. It's one thing to see a ghost on TV or in the movies; real life is a whole other ball of spirit.

Persephone and Sherlock disappear. Sage and Bis gather the items from the table and Sage tosses the candle in the can under my sink. Madam X rushes out, seemingly shaken as well, and Raven taps at her phone. "There's something odd about her," she says.

You're telling me. "Don't touch her chair," I tell all of them, "or the table where she sat."

Jones frowns, and Lia asks, "Why?"

I glance at Logan. "We need *your guy* to come raise fingerprints."

"I'm on it." He grabs his cell and shoots off a text.

Jones says nothing about that, but does ask me, "Ms. Norwalk mentioned fighting with Mr. Springer before this weekend, correct?"

I place a tea ball filled with raspberry lemon leaves in a cup of hot water. The scent instantly perks me up. "She did."

"According to what he told us, he was about to end their relationship. Is it possible she arrived at the bed and break-fast secretively, and they fought again? Perhaps she saw the note, or he told her they were through."

"Sounds plausible, and Jill did mention she heard voices."

He studies his notepad. "Mrs. Carr said she was in the bath when she heard them. Why didn't she tell me this when I interviewed her?"

At the moment, I'm more concerned with the teenager in my home. She's as pale as any ghost. Logan has taken the seat next to her, and is asking her about the movie marathon. This seems to distract her, making her smile as she tells him about her friend.

"She acted like she had forgotten about it," I tell Jones.

"I believe it's time I have another discussion with Ms. Norwalk, and perhaps Mrs. Carr, too."

"Let me know what you learn." I take the cup to Lia. "Is there anything else you need me to do?"

From his shirt pocket, he removes a small plastic bag and holds it up to the light. "Do you know what this is?"

I study the pink crystals. "Sure, bath salts." My brain sounds a warning bell. "Where did you find them?"

"During my second tour of the attic."

"Jill must've been in there after her soak in the tub."

His chin dips in agreement. "It is possible the timing of her bath could be called into question." He pockets both the crystals and his notepad, then nods at those of us left. "An interesting evening, to be sure."

He strolls out my back door, and I see him heading toward the B&B.

I rush to the porch. "What about Madam X? Do you know her real identity?"

"Not yet," he says, and keeps walking.

I curse under my breath. I swear he only brought her to irritate me.

"I'm sorry," I say to Lia, returning to sit across from her. Logan has her laughing and more like herself again, and I'm grateful to him. He reaches across the table and holds out his hand to me. I clasp it. "That was intense, and you shouldn't have had to experience such a thing."

She leans forward, expression serious. "Are you kidding? *Best day ever.* I can't wait to tell the others that I actually saw a ghost. Two of them! I heard them speak! It was epic."

I glance at Logan and his eyes are worried but he smiles. "It was definitely intense."

"I have to group chat with everybody." She takes the tea, stands, and wrestles her phone from her back pocket. As she leaves the room, Tabby follows, giving me a look that says she'll keep an eye on the girl. "Oh," Lia calls over her shoulder. "Mom said I could stay the night."

Apparently, I have no say in the matter, but I'm almost relieved. That way if she has questions or nightmares, I'll be here to help.

Logan comes around to my side and pulls me into a hug. "Was that normal?"

Raven snorts, and I can't tell if it's over the question or something on her phone.

"When you're dealing with spirits, there is no such thing," I say. "The flame, though? That was a first for me."

"Do you still think Madam X is involved with what's happened to Sage?"

Raven looks up. I scrub my face. "I don't know, but I'm not letting her off the hook. I suspect Jones isn't either. Until we have evidence she is, there's nothing we can do."

From his pocket he draws a card and shows it to me. It's one from the Zultan machine. *Consider this your warning.*

"Did it spit that out at you? When?"

"Not me. This was the one for you."

I take it and tear it in half before throwing it in the waist can. "Reverend Stout told me there's a lot of activity at Perry Buchanan's. A variety of cars coming and going all the time."

"Are you changing the subject?"

Sure am. "It's a rental now. I've got a feeling we need to see who's living there."

He pauses, waiting, I imagine, for me to go back to the Zultan prediction. When I don't, he shakes his head. "You think they could be tied to what happened at Tea Leaves?"

"Can't hurt to check, right? They didn't approach the place from the street."

"Which leaves the alley." He nods. "I get it, but we're chasing our tail. First Madam X, now this. Promise me you'll be careful."

I start to tell him I'll be fine, when Raven kicks me with her good foot under the table. When I glance at her, she clears her throat. I know what she's saying—Logan's as worried as Queenie, just not showing it outwardly. "I promise."

Sage has all her stuff packed. "Guess we'll be going. I'm spending the night at the shop. Even though my tormentor can't come onto the property, there are other ways of damaging it, and they may step up their game. The last thing

I want is for it to burn down or end up with an unexpected and unexplained gas leak."

"I'm staying with her," Bis tells us.

We walk to the display windows and Logan crosses his arms as he stares at his building. "Are the cameras working?"

"Yes," I say. "Ours are."

Sage echoes me. "Ours, too. We installed several."

Logan nods. "We'll catch them. Be safe."

Bis fist bumps him and they head across the street.

"Should we stay up and keep watch?" I ask. "Daddy's coming to dust for fingerprints. Might as well."

"You need a warm bath and some rest. Mox and I will keep an eye on things."

"If you're staying up, so am I."

He pulls me into an embrace and kisses me. I'm sort of wishing Lia *wasn't* sleeping over, but before I can voice that, the front door opens and Jones walks in.

He rocks back on his heels, looking disgusted. "Sandra Norwalk is missing."

WHILE WE SPREAD the news and Jones puts out an official alert, there's not much else we can do that night. Daddy gets a few prints and he and Jones promise to run them through the system, but the priority is finding Sandra.

Wednesday morning, Lia is no worse for wear and at home. Gloria arrives with her enormous sewing basket and a lovely smile on her face for a day of fittings. She has no idea what's been going on, and for the next few hours, I can forget about it, too, at least until Rosie comes to work and wants to know the dirt from the séance.

Gloria and Rosie don't even blink as I fill them in,

including the double timelines to give Gloria the backstory about each problem plaguing me.

When our first bride arrives, Logan takes Lia home and returns to ensconce himself in his office. No one has seen Sandra, and her car is gone from the church parking lot, suggesting she has fled town. Since that's something a guilty party would do, Jones is as angry as a bull elephant.

He did manage to interrogate Jill again, and she claimed to have no idea how the bath salts got in the third floor room. She even went so far as to suggest a mouse had deposited them there, or perhaps Sandra was trying to frame her.

After the fitting is finished, I check my voicemail to retrieve a call from Dr. Ernestine. She tells me Latimer was attacked the previous night while performing an autopsy.

I call her back. "I'm so sorry. Our ghost paid me a visit, too."

"Did you find out any new information? Why he's doing this?"

"He claims his organs were taken out, apparently against his wishes. I assume because of an autopsy, but I was wondering if there were any recent deaths where the organs were donated?"

"Sure, we've had several this past year. I may know the one you're talking about. He was involved in an accident and came to us in a coma. The attending physician declared him brain dead and, after several months, his family signed consent papers before life support was removed at their request."

"That could be our guy. I assume Dr. Latimer did the surgery?"

"There was a team, but yes, I believe he was part of it. I'll look up the file and validate it."

"That would be great. If I can get his name and confirmation of what happened, I can explain it to him."

We disconnect, and I've just finished hanging up when the phone rings. "Autopsy results are in," Jones says. "Todd Springer had several small defensive wounds on one arm, and human tissue under his fingernails. He scratched his attacker. We have DNA, now I need to find our killer. Any chance you can use your woo-woo skills to figure out where she's gone?"

"I'm not a psychic in the way you're thinking. Secondly, have you forgotten about the fact Jill's story and timeline is questionable? That you found traces of her bath salts in the attic? Her situation fits with what Todd told us. She is the half-sister, the money is his grandmother's, and Jill is trying to get it by selling off her music portfolio."

"Are you questioning me?"

Lord, help me. The man's ego is bigger than our whole state. "I'm suggesting you have a narrow focus and our real killer may get away."

He grunts and says through gritted teeth, "I'll take it from here."

I channel Mama. "Fine, but the next time you ambush me with Madam X, you and I are going to have a come-to-Jesus talk. You get what I'm saying?"

He grunts again, but this time it sounds like a laugh. Then he hangs up.

The rest of the day is uneventful, comparatively speaking. It's as if we're all holding our breath, everyone on edge, waiting for the next shoe to drop.

Helen calls and postpones our dinner, claiming she has a migraine. I'm sorry she feels unwell, but also relieved.

While Moxley snores on the rug beside us, I cuddle into

Logan's embrace on the couch that evening and enjoy a glass of wine. Try to, at least. I've had one sip when Winter phones.

"Hey, you. How are you doing?" I ask.

"The question is, how are *you*? I just finished with Sage. She told me what's going on."

I sit forward and put my glass on the coffee table. "Is she in danger?"

"Oh, Ava." She sighs heavily. "Sage is perfectly safe."

"That's great. Why do you sound so bummed?"

"Because," she says, "you're the one who's in danger."

EIGHTEEN

A chill races down my spine. I've been ignoring the omens—seems it's time to stop pretending they're not there.

Hearing Winter's proclamation, Logan goes on high alert. Mox opens his eyes. "I knew it. Any idea from who or what?" he asks her.

My friend is a powerful psychic, her sisters, too. "All I'm getting," Winter says, "is an unknown man. He seems to be close to you, yet not. I can't see who he is—it's almost as if you don't know him, but only know *of* him. Does that make sense?"

I glance at Logan. "LaCosta Hoyt. Our mysterious handyman who fixed the Zultan machine? He's about the only one I can think of."

He runs a hand over his face, looking weary. "Makes sense. This all started with Sage and that stupid carnival game. I'll track him down," he seems to say this to Winter, rather than me. "I'll keep her safe."

"Daddy's looking into him as well. Any idea why he wants to harm *me*? I seriously have no idea who he is."

"Maybe because you have a reputation for putting criminals behind bars? I don't know."

"He's obviously using an assumed name, and working with Madam X. Did you see anything about her?"

"Sage had me check her energy, too." A cat cries on Winter's end—must be the shop cat, Godfrey. Tabby races into the room to stare at the phone as Winter continues. "The woman has a protective bubble around herself. I couldn't read anything. I'm going to send you a spell to uncover if her intentions are true. It requires a piece of hair or other DNA from her. Don't take any risks to get it, but the spell is highly accurate. It's the only way I know to be sure."

"I have her fingerprints, but I don't suppose that will be enough, will it?"

Winter chuckles. "Do I want to know why you have those?"

"No," Logan and I say in unison, sharing a smile. "I'll see what I can do," I tell Winter. "Thank you."

We say our goodbyes and I grab my wine again, sinking back in the cushions. "I should call Daddy and see if he's found out anything about this guy."

"I'll call him." Logan takes my hand and draws me to my feet. "You go upstairs and draw a bath. You haven't slept well in days. I'm here, you're safe, and I'm putting you to bed early."

It's a nice thought and I take my wine. My foot hits the bottom stair when the porch screen door screeches and Brax bursts in, startling us both. Moxley comes to his feet and Arthur and Lancelot follow each other in from wherever they've been hiding.

The look on my friend's face makes me forget about my plans. "Madam X just called. There's been a break-in at The Toad. We closed it because of the memorial service. She says the place is wrecked."

Rhys trails behind him, looking shell-shocked. "We can't... I don't know what we're going to... Who would do a such a thing?"

My stomach falls and I hug him. "I'm so sorry."

"You called the police?" Logan asks.

Brax nods. "Jones is meeting us there. We have to assess the damage. Figure out if anything's been stolen."

"We'll come with you," I tell him.

"Can you watch the B&B instead? We have two guests checking in tonight, and Jones wants to keep tabs on Jill and Gordon."

"Of course," Logan says. "We'll stay as long as we're needed."

"Go." I wave them toward the door. Rhys hugs me again and I pat his back. The poor guy is going to be in the hospital with a nervous breakdown before the week is over. "It will be all right. We have each other. We've been through worse and made it. We'll get through this, too. I promise."

They leave and Logan and I clean up our glasses. The cats slink off again and Mox follows us. "You know how to check people in?"

I shrug. "How hard can it be? Besides, I want to get a look at the piano. There's a reason Todd felt pulled to it. I want to know what it is."

"You still need to be careful," he reminds me. "You said yourself that the killer is on the loose. Let's not provoke whoever it is."

Leaving the dog behind, we cross the kitchen and hit the

porch. "I can't see Jill shoving someone to their death. Especially a big guy like Todd. I wish I could have asked him why he was in the attic in the first place."

Next door, we let ourselves in, and discover Jill and Gordon coming downstairs with their suitcases.

"You're checking out?" I ask. "Rhys didn't mention you were leaving."

"We were only booked through tonight," Gordon says. "Our vacation was ruined, and that detective has his autopsy results. No reason for us to stay."

How had they found out about the autopsy? Has Jones given them permission to leave? With insufficient evidence against them, I have to assume he couldn't hold them any longer.

Jill keeps avoiding my eyes and glancing out the front parlor window. "I'll be in touch about the party. After giving it some thought, I'm not sure the vineyard is the best place for it. I need to think about it, talk to my grandmother."

Desperation to keep them here gnaws at me, but what can I do? Gordon opens the door and sets the luggage on the veranda. I trail after them. "You're sure you didn't know Todd?"

Both of them jerk their heads toward me. "Why does everyone keep asking us that?" Gordon huffs. It's obviously a rhetorical question, and he doesn't wait for me to answer. "We never met the man before. Whatever is going on in that crazy head of yours, let it go."

Logan gets in his face. "There's no reason to be rude."

I take his hand, pull him back. "It's okay."

Jill grips the handle of her suitcase tightly. "Instead of harassing us, you should be trying to find Sandra. If there was foul play involved, she was the cause of it."

She stomps off the porch, heading for their car. Gordon picks up their stuff, prepared to follow. "We definitely won't be having Grams' party here, and you can be sure that I will put a scathing review on Yelp for this place."

He tosses their suitcases in the backseat, Jill already inside and waiting. Before he can climb in, however, Sandra steps from the side of the house. "If there was foul play involved," she mimics Jill's words, "I was *not* the cause of it. But I know who was."

Logan and I watch in horror as Sandra raises a handgun and points it at Gordon.

Jill screams in the car. Gordon freezes, hands going into the air. His face is a mixture of shock and fear. "What in the world do you think you're doing?"

"There were only two people, besides Brax and Rhys, here that night. Detective Jones believes it was me that shoved Todd out that window, but it was you. You're lying about not knowing him. What did he ever do to you? Why would you kill him?"

Logan takes a step off the porch and I grab his arm, trying to hold him here. "Sandra, why don't y'all come inside and let's talk about this."

He's unmovable, so I step down beside him, keeping my hand around his arm. "Logan's right. This been a horrible trauma, especially for you, Sandra. We want to find the killer as much as you do, but shooting Gordon isn't the answer."

"Why did I have to argue with him right before he came here?" Sandra's voice hitches. "I was supposed to come with him, but no, I had to put my job first because I was angry with him. If I'd been here, maybe I could've prevented his death."

I think about the breakup note. Does she know? "You can't blame yourself," I tell her. "You had no idea this would happen."

A tear slips down her cheek. "Doesn't matter. I was all he had in this world, and I was too selfish to put him first. I should have appreciated him more."

From the corner of my eye, I notice Jill shifting around. Gordon still has his hands in the air. I glance across the street to Tea Leaves, hoping that maybe Sage, Bis, or Raven have seen us and called Jones. This could go bad very quickly.

"We all feel that way when it comes to our loved ones," I offer.

Todd appears, his ghost hovering near Jill's side of the car. "You need to get Sandra out of here," he says in a shaky voice.

"Todd is here now, Sandra," I tell her. "I am a psychic medium, and I can speak to the dead."

Startled by this revelation, she blinks and the hand with the gun lowers. She peers around with wild eyes. "He is? He's a ghost?"

"He's going to help us figure out exactly what happened." I take another step down, only to feel Logan's strong hand gripping my bicep.

"Ava," he says under his breath, "What are you doing?"

Trying to stop another murder. "Tell him what you just said to me," I coach her. "He can hear you."

"Todd?" Her voice trembles and she dashes another tear from her cheek. "Can you really hear me?"

The ghost faces me. "Get her out of here!"

Persephone is suddenly present and points to Jill. "Look out!"

The woman shoves open her door and emerges with a

look of scorn on her face. A revolver in hand, she faces Sandra. "How dare you accuse us of killing him!"

Logan pushes me up onto the veranda as Jill's gun goes off.

I tumble to the floorboards, hearing Sandra cry out. Todd yells at me, Gordon screams at Jill. Another shot rings through the air, and I flinch. Logan throws himself over me.

"Put that weapon down, y'hear now? You don't wanna shoot anybody else."

The voice is familiar, but unfortunately, it's not Detective Jones. I peek out from under Logan's arm and see a woman who resembles Madam X standing in the driveway. She appears unarmed, but on second glance, I notice something in her right hand.

Logan raises up enough for us to watch as Jill whirls on her, both hands holding her weapon. She's shaking from head to toe. "Who are you?"

Gordon stares bewildered at Sandra, crumpled on the lawn. "What have you done?" he hisses at his wife. "Get in the car. We have to get out of here. Now!"

"I'm afraid I can't let you do that," Madam X says. She looks different. No makeup and her hair is cropped short to her head. She must have been previously wearing a wig. The gaudy jewelry is missing, too, as well as her long skirt. She's dressed in jeans, a T-shirt, and sneakers. A totally different person. "Sandra is wrong. Todd's death is my fault. I am the one who set up this meeting, hoping you would see that Mr. Springer only wanted a family. He didn't care about your grandmother's portfolio, or the millions it's valued at, Jill. Or should I say, Marni?"

Jill's face pales, but her arms steady. She aims at Madam X. "How do you know that?"

The psychic starts to reach for her back pocket and Jill cocks the gun. Madam X stops. "I'm just going for my business card. My name is Kit Lyons. I'm a private detective. Todd hired me to find his mom and dad."

She certainly fooled me. Her getup as a psychic had also fooled Todd's ghost at the séance.

"After I tracked down the real Jill's father," she continues, "he died before the two of them had a chance to meet. Todd was a nice guy but had the worst luck of anyone I ever met. He went into a tailspin, believing he wasn't meant to find his family, but I made sure he reached out to you. You rejected him, of course, out of your own greed, and he sunk even lower."

Todd hovers over Sandra, and I motion to Logan. "We need to help her," I whisper.

Stay here, he mouths, pointing to the spot. Gordon and Jill are staring at Kit. Logan shifts away from me and cautiously eases down the steps and over to Sandra.

Gordon grits his teeth and sneers at Kit. "Greed? He was a con man, pretending to be her long lost brother. What a joke. He wanted in on the money."

Nothing in her expression changes. She appears completely neutral, and unafraid of the gun pointed at her. "He had the DNA results. All you had to do was take one yourself and verify that he's your brother," she says to Jill. "But of course, he's not, is he? And you know why."

"Those can be falsified." Her hands are shaking again, but her face was fierce. She took a step toward the woman. "I've read about it. These con artists fleece you for everything you're worth."

"It's not your money, Marni. It belongs to Teresa, who is Todd's grandmother, and not yours." Genuine sadness shows in her eyes. "He wanted to meet her, get to know her. After your rejection, I started digging into you two." She motions at the couple. "Found out you were going to be here this weekend, so I insisted that Todd come, as well. I didn't know who you really were yet, and I assured him a vacation in this beautiful town would do him and Sandra good. It would give him a chance to convince you he had only the best of intentions. Unfortunately, you didn't."

Jill swallows hard. "You said he was going to sign a statement declaring he wasn't related to me."

Kit smiles. "The interesting fact is, he wasn't. The only fleecing going on here is that you are not related to Teresa Bird, at all. My investigation took a very interesting turn a few days ago when I discovered what you'd done, who you really are."

"We have no idea what you're talking about," Gordon sneers.

"Rayland Cease and Marni Mayfield. I have to give you credit, the long con was going to work for you. I can't figure out how you knew that portfolio would be worth so much down the road, but maybe that's not what you were after to begin with."

Jill's arms are getting tired from holding the revolver. "You're insane. You have no idea what you're talking about. Teresa Bird is my grandmother. I deserve my portion of that money."

From the corner of my eye, I see Logan removing his phone from his pocket and pushing buttons. I assume he's calling 911. Todd hovers over Sandra, talking too softly for me to hear and trying to stroke her head and face. His phantom fingers go right through her, and he cries his frustration.

Gordon, a.k.a. Rayland, glares at his co-conspirator over the top of the car. "Great. Look at what you've gotten us into now. Shoot her. We've got to scram."

Who uses that word these days? It cements the idea that he's similar to some old-timey con man.

Kit takes a step closer, that calm smile not faltering. "Your granddad put you up to this, didn't he, Rayland? He knew Teresa back in the day, and he certainly exploited and swindled plenty of folks in his time, didn't he?"

The man walks around the front of the vehicle to stand beside Marnie. "There's a sucker born every minute. It was the first lesson he taught me."

Sandra sucks in a loud gasp of air, and we all swivel to look at her. Logan has laid his cell on the grass, and is pressing his shirt into a wound on her side. "You've been shot," he tells her in a composed tone, his faint Southern accent rolling off his tongue like warm butter. "Don't you worry. You're going to be fine."

Marni screeches as Rayland rips the weapon from her and marches toward the two of them. "Over my dead body," he snarls.

"Ava!" Persephone cries.

I launch myself off the porch and onto the man, a shot ringing out in the hot summer night.

NINETEEN

Everything happens at once. Colliding with Rayland, the two of us hit the ground. Marni screams and kicks me in the ribs. At the same time, her accomplice elbows me in the nose.

Searing pain causes my eyes to tear. Fighting my suddenly blurry vision, I grab his wrist, attempting to push his gun hand to the ground. Blood runs from my nose and splatters his shirt.

He outweighs me and flips me off, breaking my hold. Marni goes stiff as a board and falls flat on her face next to us, startling Rayland. Kit stands over her, the device in her hand connecting two wires to Marni's back. A stun gun. "If you'd stayed put, Ava, I could have zapped him. When you're flailing around like that, I can't fire in case I hit you!"

Rayland pushes off me. Ears ringing and twinkling lights on the edge of my vision, I sit up and scramble to grab him, but the frozen Marni is in my way. Logan yells my name as Rayland rises to his feet and aims at my face.

The night sky is a backdrop to his bulky frame and my

limbs feel like hundred pound weights. I attempt to haul myself over the flattened woman. My hand slips on her silky shirt and I crash down onto her. "No, don't—" I start to say, fear coursing through my veins.

A body comes from the side, tackles Rayland, and takes him to the ground.

The gun goes off, a bullet skimming past my cheek and lodging in the side of the porch.

My husband, now on top of the man, punches him in the nose, wrestles the weapon from his grip, and then clocks him with the butt of it. Rayland's eyes roll up in his head and he's out.

"Nice work." Kit steps over me and Marni. "I wasn't going to let him shoot her, you know."

Breathing hard, Logan gives her a hard look. "You have some explaining to do."

She raises her hands in contrition. "I do. First, let's tie these two up for Detective Jones and get Sandra to the hospital."

Sage and Bis come rushing to us. Bis is carrying a fire poker; Sage, a broom. Both appear ready to swing first and ask questions later. Raven, on the porch of Tea Leaves, waves her phone. "I called the police!"

Logan lifts me from Marni and cradles me in his arms. "You couldn't stay put, could you?"

Smiling hurts and I taste coppery blood on my tongue. "He was going to shoot you."

Sherlock appears and leans over, studying my face. "I dare say, Ava, you've broken your nose."

. . .

THE THORNHOLLOW CLINIC is closed this late, so I
end up at the hospital, along with Sandra. Dr. Ernestine is
on duty, and Logan and I wait in an ER exam room until
she's free. His chastising takes on the form of a lecture at one
point, but I keep silent and nod at appropriate intervals. He
could give Mama a run for her money, but I have plenty of
experience being on the end of her wrath, and learned a long
time ago there was no use arguing.

I feel my actions were justified, but I understand his
need to vent. I regularly scare the bejesus out of him, as he
repeatedly states while he paces, and I know fear is driving
his exasperation.

Sage and Bis are watching the B&B, but because it's the
scene of another crime, Detective Jones has made them turn
away the two new guests. Calls come in from my parents, as
well as Brax, interrupting him while I assure them I'm okay.
The second I disconnect with each, Logan starts up again.

Once he runs out of steam, he holds my hand, and
doesn't turn loose, even when the doctor gives me a localized
anesthetic and realigns my nose. She packs the nostrils with
gauze, then brings me up-to-date on Avenger as she writes a
script for pain medication. "I looked up our possible organ
donor and can confirm his heart and one kidney were
removed. Everything was above board—all the paperwork
was signed. What can we do to get him to stop terrifying Dr.
Latimer?"

My voice sounds like I have a head cold when I speak. "I
have an idea, but it will require cooperation from his family."
I fill her in on my plan, and since certain laws require she not
share the patient's name or family contact information, she
agrees to act as a liaison. She suspects they'll think she's
crazy to suggest my idea, but she wants her morgue back to

normal. "Saturday night, again?" she asks, handing me the prescription.

Logan takes it from her and shoves it in his back pocket. "Can it wait? As you can see, Ava's been through a lot this week."

"It's okay," I tell him. "I can handle it, but if the family doesn't agree to this," I shrug at Dr. Ernestine, "I'm afraid I'm out of solutions."

She walks for the door. "I'll get them there. Take care of that nose."

"I don't like it," Logan says.

I squeeze his hand. "Let's play it by ear, okay? You can come with me, if it makes you feel better."

Rhys rushes to us when Logan and I discover him and Brax in the waiting room. "Heavens to Betsy," he says, pulling me into a gentle hug. "You were supposed to check in the guests, not get yourself shot at."

Brax takes his turn in the hug department, squeezing me for all he's worth. "You scared us to death. What were you thinking?"

"She was trying to save me," Logan says, that edge of chastisement in his tone again. "I honestly don't know what to do with her."

"A loving thank you seems in order." I smile at his scowl. "I can think of several ways you can show your appreciation once we're home." This lightens the mood just enough, making my friends laugh and him fight to keep from smiling...or maybe that look means he wants to pinch me. Or spank me. I'm not sure, and I don't care. I lean into him and he puts an arm around me. "Like Queenie, when someone threatens my family, I get mad."

He kisses my forehead. "You're incorrigible."

"Yes, I am. You better get used to it."

Sandra is patched up and Jones is taking her statement when we stop to visit her. The doctor is keeping her overnight, saying she's exhausted physically, as well as emotionally. It seems like a good idea.

When she sees me and my swollen nose, she stretches out a hand. "Oh, my goodness gracious, are you all right?"

I take it. "I'll be fine. How are you?"

"The bullet passed right through. I'll be going home tomorrow." She releases me and says to Logan, "Thank you."

Jones is reading over his notes. "You two wait outside. I'll take your statements in a moment."

I feel as exhausted as Sandra. "Madam X—a.k.a. Kit Lyons—is who you need to talk to. She's a private investigator and can tell you all about Marni and Rayland, as well as what happened at the B&B. We're going home, and will give you our statements tomorrow."

I wink at Sandra and head for the door, dragging Logan with me.

Jones huffs. "You could have gotten yourself killed, Fantome. Why didn't you just call me?"

I stop and look over my shoulder. "It's Fantome-Cross, and I had to stop Rayland from killing Sandra or Logan, and Marni from doing the same to Kit. You've got your bad guys, and the rest of us are okay. A few words of gratitude might be nice."

He pockets his notepad and crosses his arms. "Marni Mayfield is wanted in three states. Rayland Cease in five. They've been lying low for years, and now we know why. They tricked poor Ms. Bird into believing Marni was her granddaughter. The real Jill and her mother left the country twenty years ago when Jill was just a girl, and have been estranged from Ms. Bird all that time. I've been in contact with her and them. They didn't even know about the death of Jill and Todd's father. Seems a family reunion is in their future. Thought you might want to know."

This is good news, and Jones' way of saying thank you. Teresa will be reunited with the real Jill, her true heir, meaning she and her mother can support Teresa learning about the loss of her grandson. "You did all that in the past hour?"

"PI Lyons already had the information and was gracious enough to share it with me."

"I'm sure she was." After he threatened to throw her in jail for withholding information, I'd bet. "She was trying to help Todd. Go easy on her."

The corners of his eyes wrinkle as he pins me with one of his stares. "That's what she said about you."

"You knew who she was at the séance, didn't you?"

"I had my suspicions."

"Why didn't you tell me?"

"I suspected she wasn't who she claimed to be, I did not expect that she was an undercover PI behind the whole situation."

"Have you spoken to Marni and Rayland? Did they confess?"

"PI Lyons arrived in time to record most of your discussion with them. I have no doubts they'll come clean when I play it for them during my interrogation. They've been working together a long time, but I suspect they will turn on each other in a heartbeat."

Good. "I'm pressing charges."

He gives me a brief smile. "I hoped you would."

Back home, I keep thinking about Todd and his grandmother. How if things had been different, maybe he'd learned to play the piano from her. That maybe he had inherited her voice. I imagine him sitting at Brax and Rhys' and filling their house with music. "I need to go next door," I tell Logan.

"We just got home."

"I've got a feeling."

"Lord woman. You'll be the death of me."

I sure hope not.

Persephone joins us as we cross the backyard. "Glad you're okay. Be sure to look inside."

She vanishes before I can reply. "I intend to," I call into the night. The crickets and tree frogs pause in their song and Logan gives me a look. "Don't ask," I say.

Inside the parlor, I run my fingers over the keys. As a girl, Mama insisted I take lessons, but I was so bad at them, she finally decided it wasn't the worth the money. Tuning would definitely improve the old Baldwin, but as I start with middle C and work my way to the right, it's the F note that sounds dull, muffled. "We need to look inside," I tell Logan.

He hefts the lid. The lighting is soft in here and I shine my phone flashlight into the space. The beam catches on a stuffed animal—one that's worn and ratty. The material covering it has faded through the years, and an eye is missing. Still, there's no doubt what it is.

A bird. Once a brightly colored parakeet, if my guess is correct.

Removing it, I show it to Logan. "Todd's?" he asks.

I nod. "Why stuff it in here?"

He shrugs. "No clue."

"Because." The ghost in question floats a few feet away, staring at it. "It was the only thing I had that connected me to my birth family. The boy left on the church steps with nothing but a blanket and a stuffed animal. I kept it all those years, my one connection to them, but also, proof of who I am. When they searched for my relatives, they put my picture with it in all the local papers before placing me up for adoption. Kit found a copy. It was a symbol of my heritage. At the time, I didn't know, but once she discovered who I was, I knew it was visual proof that my mother had sent me a message. I just never realized it pointed to my real last name."

"Why hide it?"

He motions at the thing. "There's a seam in the back. Open it."

I see a section of material where it's been opened and resewed by hand. The poor bird is so old and worn, it takes little effort to tear it, the fabric around the tiny, careful stitches fraying. I realize it's been opened and repaired more than once.

"When I was six, I discovered it had that hidden pocket," Todd says. "I didn't understand the significance of what it held."

There is indeed, a satin pouch. It's held together with a ribbon. Setting down the stuffed animal, I carefully open it. A rolled up black and white photo of Teresa Bird is faded and creased, but I recognize her striking features from the one Marni showed me. "Your grandmother."

He nods. "And that." He motions at a cassette tape. "I believe it's her voice. An angel's voice. I thought the lullaby on it was all for me. I kept it hidden but listened to it as often as I could. When I discovered Teresa was my grandmother, it made sense. I think my mother recorded her singing, prob- ably without her knowing it, and stuffed it inside the bag with the photo. Another clue. When I bought her albums a few months ago, it was the same voice."

"And you realized that if Marni, impersonating Jill, got hold of it..." Logan says.

"She could destroy it," Todd finishes. "I couldn't let that happen. I needed to be sure it was safe."

The stuffing in the bird had taken a beating, but it had saved the tape from damage. I return it and the photo to the satin bag. "Who do you want me to see gets this?"

"My grandmother. I want her to know that her voice saved me many, many times when I was young. I listened to that whenever I felt lost. I want her to know I'm sorry I didn't get to meet her, but that I'm watching over her and the real Jill."

"I'll make sure she gets the tape, and the message."

"Thank you," he says. "And tell them not to be sad. I've met my mom and dad here in heaven." He smiles. "I'm with my family after all these years."

Tears press against the back of my eyes. "I'm so happy for you."

And then he's gone.

TWENTY

Saturday morning I have two black eyes for the christening, although the swelling of my nose has gone down considerably. I look like a raccoon who lost a bar fight.

No amount of makeup will cover it completely, although Brax and Sage do their best to minimize it.

Rayland and Marni are cooling their heels in jail, their bail hearing on hold until Monday, due to Judge Barlow coming down with a stomach bug. His usual fill-in is on a cruise in Alaska, and others from surrounding counties are too busy to stand in. The two have claimed violation of their rights and due process, blah blah blah, but there's literally nothing that can be done at the moment.

According to Jones, Marni gave up her partner, explaining how he did hear Todd speaking to a woman the night he died—Kit. He'd gone to the attic, hoping, it seemed, for more privacy. Rayland had snuck into his room to look for the DNA results, saw the break up letter, and had the brilliant idea to make it look like he'd committed suicide.

Todd had just hung up when Rayland confronted him. Rayland was friendly, gaining his trust and forcing the window open. He pretended they were all going to be a big, happy family, got Todd to join him at the window to look at the view, and then shoved him out.

Daddy shows up right before lunch, scratching Moxley behind his big ears, and giving me a big hug before he turns to my friend. "Glad you're here," he tells Sage. "I've discovered the identity of your culprit."

We gather in the kitchen and he lays out a grainy, black and white security camera photograph alongside a mugshot of a man. "LaCosta Hoyt is actually Cosmine LaHoyt. Criminals think they're so smart when they create an anagram of their name." He rolls his eyes and it reminds me of me. "A thumbprint I lifted from the machine matches those in the system. Recognize him?"

Sage fingers it. "That's the guy who broke into the Emporium when I was in high school. Mom was running it then. He stole hundreds of dollars of jewelry from us, and the police caught him before he got down the road, thanks to my mother's Bewilder spell." When we all give her a blank look, she explains. "It causes a thief to become disoriented if they steal from you and try to make a getaway."

Handy. Daddy fishes out his reading glasses and rattles off facts from his phone. "Since he was caught red-handed, he went to prison for six years. Just got out a few weeks ago." He taps the security camera photo. "Came to town shortly after that."

She squints at the black and white shot. "That doesn't look anything like him."

"Thanks to six years of aging, forty pounds more weight, and a bit of reconstructive surgery on his face. One of the other inmates took a knife to him, going for his eye, but missed. The injury did damage to his cheekbone, fracturing it." He pockets the cell and removes his glasses. "Do you recognize the background in that shot?"

This time, she holds it up. "Is that the library next to Chicks With Gifts?"

"It is. A few days after he got out. I suspect he tried to get inside your Emporium again."

Her face slackens and she drops the picture. "The ladder. The one Raven fell from. She found it outside, leaning against the wall. We thought someone had dropped it off, like a donation. A weird one, but sometimes folks don't know what to do with stuff and figure we'll find it a new home. It seemed like a good, solid ladder, and we decided to keep it, rather than resell it. Do you think he was trying to break in?"

I think of her sister's ankle. "He tampered with it. He's the cause of Raven's injury."

She curses him under her breath. "And he learned about me opening the tea shop, so he came here and tried to harm me, too."

"Revenge," Brax comments. Arthur has suckered him into picking him up, and purrs inside his beefy arms. "Clever way to do it."

"Bold but stupid." Sage's face is hard, her eyes unforgiving. "He figured I wouldn't recognize him, and he was right. He stood right there and acted like he was helping me."

She's blaming herself, and I know that feeling. I give her arm a quick squeeze. "How do we find him?" I ask Daddy.

"Landon wants to issue an APB for him in both towns, but I talked him out of it."

"Why?" Sage and I chorus.

"My guess is he's here in Thornhollow. He'll be keeping tabs on his police scanner and we don't want to tip him off that we know. He'll disappear and make the job of catching him even harder."

"So what can we do?" Brax asks. "Sit around and wait for him to strike again?"

"Don't you worry." Daddy pats Sage's shoulder. "I'll sniff him out before he can do more harm. He'll be in jail again before he can blink."

Sage has regained her normal color and I recognize the glower in her eyes. "I know how to find him. I'll get you a location."

"That's not necessary," Daddy says, and then he realizes her meaning—she's going to use her magic to track the guy down. "But if you get any leads, let me know."

She disappears into the living room, where Bis is talking to Logan. The business phone rings and I ignore it, but I hear Lia answer as I walk Daddy out.

"It's for you," she says, holding out the landline's receiver. "Some lady named Teresa."

Teresa Bird? Daddy follows me into the office. I take the phone. "This is Ava."

"Mrs. Fantome-Cross? My name is Teresa Bird." Her voice is frail and wavers slightly. "I believe you know who I am. May I have a moment of your time, if I could impose? My granddaughter, Jill—the real Jill—and I would like to say thank you."

"Yes, ma'am." I put her on speaker. "It's nice to meet you. I listened to some of your music yesterday. You're extremely talented."

Having overheard the conversation, Sage, Bis, and Logan join us.

A heavy sigh echoes from the speaker. "And now, I'm very blind. In more ways than physical sight. Those two took advantage of me, and cost me my grandson."

A second voice cuts in. "He was truly related to us, right?"

I assume this is Jill. "The private detective he hired has all the documentation, and I have a gift Todd asked me to give you." I explain about the stuffed bird with the lullaby tucked inside. "He listened to your voice many times during the years, not knowing who you were, but believing you were an angel watching over him. Now, he's watching over you."

There's crying and it's both sad and joyful. At least they have this to hang onto.

"With your permission, I'll send the bird and its contents to you via my pastor." I've already spoken to Reverend Stout and it was his idea. "He and his wife are the ones who found Todd on the church steps. They wanted to adopt him, but fate intervened."

"Thank you," Teresa says through her tears. "I'm setting up a memorial in Todd's name with a grant for young musicians. It will be my legacy, but also his."

"What a wonderful idea. I'm sure he'd love it."

Jill speaks up. "You sound like you know him."

Here goes nothing. "I'm a medium," I admit. There's a pregnant silence from their end. "He's been in contact after his death. That's how I know."

"Sandra told us," Teresa says. "I never believed in such things before, but I do now. We're getting together when Jill and her mother return to the States. Sandra has promised to tell all of us about him."

Phew. *Thank you, Sandra.* That went easier than I anticipated. "That's wonderful. I hear you have a birthday coming up in November. If you need a place to hold a party, let me know. I've already reserved the Cross Vineyard, if you're interested, and my fees are on the house."

"I'll think about it. We've lost much, but we've also gained a new closeness. Maybe I should celebrate."

"Definitely. We'll be in touch," Jill says. "Thanks again."

We disconnect and Lia claps. "What a great story! I can't wait to put this on my vlog!"

LATER, at the christening, the photographer looks flustered at my appearance. With the layers of concealer and foundation, I'd thought I might pass for simply looking sleep deprived, but his horrified face lets me know I'm a nightmare. "I'll have to charge extra for photoshopping," he tells Rosie, still staring at me.

"Photoshopping?" she echoes, indignant.

He transforms his features, becoming the consummate professional again. "While I'm at it, I can plump her lips,"—a hand flutters over my face—"and take a smidge off her jawline to soften it. Perhaps shrink that large forehead."

I'm speechless. *Large forehead?*

"You most certainly will not," Rosie says, handing my goddaughter to her husband. She grabs the photographer's waving hand and turns him around, marching him down the church's aisle. "Your services are no longer needed."

He argues but she continues to parade him out, only allowing him to gather his equipment.

"Do I have a large forehead?" I ask Logan, touching it.

He kisses me above the brows. "You're perfect."

"Can you believe the nerve of that guy?" Rosie asks when she returns. She brushes her hands as if she's gotten them dirty by touching him. "He asked to be placed on our suggested vendor list to brides, so I thought I'd see if he was a good fit by hiring him for this. Yeesh! What a moron."

I can't help running my fingers over my jawline. "He might have made our brides feel inadequate, so it's good we didn't add him, but maybe he has a point. I should skip being in the pictures. I don't want to ruin them."

Lia bombs up to me, a goofy smile on her face. She's wearing a lovely pink dress with a ribbon sash, and Mrs. Chen waves from one of the pews. I've never seen Lia in anything but jeans. "Why would you ruin the pictures? I think you look badass."

"Lia," I admonish, glancing around to make sure Reverend Stout hasn't heard her swear.

"You're a warrior." She strikes a pose like she has a sword and is fighting off monsters. "Defender of good." *Slash.* "Defeating evil where it exists." *Slash.* "Saving ordinary mortals and the spirits of the unjustly murdered!"

She continues her imaginary battle, drawing the attention of the crowd. Most smile, egging her on. When Sage and Bis arrive, they take seats beside Mrs. Chen and Lia plunks down next to them.

Mama and Daddy hail me from the back. When I join them, Mama frowns at my face, but hugs me. "You look lovely."

Liar. "As do you," I reply.

"Can you come for dinner?"

"I'm afraid I have other plans. Brunch tomorrow?"

"Absolutely." Daddy kisses my *large forehead.*

Sage appears at my side and tells Daddy, "I used my pendulum over a map of the town and LaHoyt is in the neighborhood."

Organ notes echo through the nave, alerting us it's time to start. Reverend Stout takes his place at the front and Rosie and her family begin to gather around the baptismal font. She looks back and waves at me.

"Do you have an exact location?" Daddy asks.

Sage shakes her head. "You don't need to leave to hunt him down. We'll get him after the party."

Daddy lifts a brow to me. I shrug. "She knows what she's doing."

"Okay," he says. "If you're sure he won't get away in the meantime."

Rosie is practically apocalyptic. I hurry, with Logan, to join them.

All goes well, and I even allow myself to be photographed. In reality, I don't have much of a choice, since Rosie enlists the entire gathered congregation of thirty people to use their phones to snap impromptu shots, as well as posed ones.

By the time we walk and head for Tea Leaves for the reception, I've smiled so much my entire face throbs. I pray my nose won't end up crooked once it heals, but I'm happy and relaxed for the first time in a week.

I have a few hours before I'm due at the hospital to speak to Avenger's family and try to cross him over. Mrs. Chen insists Lia needs to attend. I hate to admit it, but I think she's right. If all goes well, the teen will get a form of closure, just like our ghost, and hopefully won't be scarred by the traumatic incident at the séance.

Logan and I are walking hand in hand behind Brax and Rhys. Sage and Bis are with Mama and Daddy, Sage in conversation with him. The expression on his face suggests he's skeptical of whatever she's telling him, but nods and continues listening.

The asphalt of the street radiates heat, clinging to my skin after the coolness of the church. Humidity weighs on my chest, making it hard to breathe. We pass the sidewalk and form a line as we go through the narrow alley next to the house that sits behind the shop. The west side of it is trees and overgrown bushes that wrap around the end of the cul-de-sac. My mind instantly imagines LaHoyt carrying the Zultan machine through this narrow space to reach the building. I can't believe one man could do it. "He had to have help," I say to Logan. "But who?"

Knowing me as well as he does, he picks up on my train of thought without needing explanation. "Give it a rest, Ava. Your dad will figure it out and catch him. If LaHoyt had an accomplice, he'll catch him, too."

As we emerge, the small parking lot at the back of Tea Leaves comes into sight. LaHoyt lies on the ground, twitching and making tiny noises of pain, as though he's having a seizure.

"That's him," I say, nudging Logan. "That's the man harassing Sage."

We hurry forward, the others gathering in a circle to watch as tiny pustules on his skin burst and his facial muscles twitch. His fingers are curled into claws, and his legs jerk randomly.

Sage smiles down at him. "You should have learned the first time, never mess with a witch."

"What did you do to him?" Daddy asks, looking wary and taking out his phone. He hits a button.

She wiggles her fingers in the air, her grin cocky. "I know how to get revenge, too."

Daddy's call goes through, and as he walks a few feet away, I hear him tell Jones that he's caught LaHoyt. They exchange a few more words and Daddy disconnects, returning to us.

The man on the ground is still wiggling, new boils breaking out on various places of exposed skin. His eyes have begun to cross. "Help...me," he croaks.

"Is he going to die?" Lia asks.

"I don't kill people," Sage says matter-of-factly, "but he won't mess with us again."

Good to know.

"What about his partner?" I look around. "I'm sure he had one."

Reverend Stout has caught up with us and studies the man lying at our feet. "Oh my. What did he run into?"

"A jinx," Sage says. When the pastor gives her a condemning look, she shrugs. "Sometimes you have to go Old Testament to protect yourself and your loved ones."

Reluctantly, Stout nods. "Amen to that." He glances over his shoulder at the alley. "He's one of the two men living in Buchanan's rental."

Daddy and I exchange a glance. "I believe we've found his partner, Ava."

TWENTY-ONE

LaHoyt and Nijar Omar are both arrested that afternoon.

The two thieves met in prison and Omar had agreed to help LaHoyt harass Sage in exchange for LaHoyt helping him break into The Thorny Toad.

Apparently, Omar had been looking for stolen cash he'd once hidden in an upstairs bedroom when it was still the flower shop. He'd worked a few months for Betty years ago, and disappeared without notice shortly after.

Kit, who is indeed psychic, helped Jones and Daddy locate the money in an air duct. The woman it belonged to, a girlfriend of Omar's, is contacted and relieved to discover he'd been caught.

That night at the hospital, Lia and I sit down with Dr. Ernestine, Dr. Latimer, our ghost's sister, and a couple with four young children. Avenger is actually Ralph Detweiler. All these people using other names makes my head spin.

I'm relieved to have brought my protégé, who immediately befriends the kids. While she entertains them in the playroom next door, I explain what's happening due to Ralph, aka Avenger, being stuck on this plane, to his sister, as well as Mr. and Mrs. Hatch.

None of them are demonstrative folks, and I can't tell at first whether they believe in ghosts or not.

Dr. Latimer is uncomfortable discussing his experiences, as well, but confirms what I tell them about the hauntings occurring in the morgue.

"That's a lot to take in," Mr. Hatch says, shifting in his chair. "Don't get me wrong, I'm certainly grateful to the man." He says this to Ralph's sister. "I needed a heart and a kidney, and they had to be from the same donor, which put us in a bit of a pickle. I'd been at the top of the waiting list for four months, and my doctors said I didn't have much longer."

His wife threads her fingers through his. Her eyes glint with unshed tears. "It was a miracle. Everything has gone pretty well since, too, which is another one. We owe that to you."

Ralph's sister gives a sad smile. "My brother wasn't perfect, that's for sure, but he was a decent guy. Had a big heart. I don't know why he's putting up a fuss about all this, but his death was a shock to our family. Certainly must've been to him."

"I know this is far outside the norm," I coax, "but if you could bear with me for a few minutes, and do as I instruct, we can bring peace to the departed so he'll cross to the afterlife. We owe him that."

The Hatches exchange a glance. I'm afraid for a moment that they're going to get up and walk out. They're clearly not interested in talking to a ghost.

Under the table, I cross my fingers, and allow them to think it over. Ralph's sister appears undisturbed by all this, and I feel I can count on her. That may have to be enough.

Miracle of miracles, as if finished with their silent conversation, the husband and wife nod, seemingly resigned. "Guess it can't hurt," Mr. Hatch says.

Dr. Latimer looks like he's enormously relieved. So am I. "We can leave the children with Dr. Ernestine. Your donor tends to hang out in the morgue, and I know that's the worst place ever to ask you to go to with me, but it's our best option to get him to speak to us tonight."

They stare at me as if I've lost my mind. "The morgue," Mrs. Hatch says, horrified.

People fear the idea of death, and I don't blame them for finding the whole thing disagreeable. My work with spirits has given me a different perspective on the afterlife, and tonight, I'm Avenger's advocate. It's not a role I would choose, but it's the one I've got. He deserves peace. Dr. Latimer does, too. "There's nothing to be scared of. We'll make it quick and get you on your way home. Please, this is really important. He did give you a second chance at life."

My guilt card has weight. Mr. Hatch steals himself and rises, pulling his wife's hand so she stands, as well. "We'll follow you."

Lia brings my bag and we retrace our steps from the previous Saturday night. The others gather off to the side, nervously watching as I take a deep breath.

"I need to get a life," I mutter. "Who spends Saturday nights in the morgue?"

She laughs and elbows me before turning on her EMF meter. "I can't think of a better place to be."

"You're weird, you know that?"

"Better than being normal." She makes an expression like she's gagging.

I suppose there's some truth to that.

Persephone and Sherlock appear, and I instantly feel better. "He'll show," Sherlock tells me with a wink. "I have made sure of it."

His gift of being able to cross back and forth with ease, together with his desire to help, is always welcome. I give him a smile, making a note to thank him properly later when I don't have an audience. I'm not performing a full-on séance as we did for Todd, only hoping my method with these folks, who have a direct connection with him, will work.

"Ralph," I call. "Your sister is here to talk to you, and I want you to meet the man who received your donated organs."

Nothing happens. "Don't worry," Lia tells them. "Ava knows what she's doing."

I'll need to thank her later, too. "Avenger," I try again with his elected name, "this is your chance to voice your feelings and get closure. Don't blow it."

My directness causes all eyes to skip to me with surprise. Maybe Kit is right—I need to be more gentle. Something to think about, but I don't want to lose my audience, who look like they want to bolt. I give the group a reassuring smile. "Ghosts are similar to kids—sometimes you have to raise your voice to get their attention."

"Will we be able to see him?" the sister asks.

"Probably not," I tell her. "I'll repeat whatever he tells me, and he'll be able to hear and see you."

The temperature suddenly plummets. "Lori?" The ghost

of the hour becomes visible, staring at his sibling. "What are you doing here?"

Hearing her has done the trick. I offer her an encouraging nod. "He's here. Talk to him. He needs to know it was your decision, but that you didn't mean to upset him."

"Ralph?" A tear slips down her cheek. "I miss you so much. I'm so sorry about what happened, and that we didn't have a chance to say goodbye. I wanted your legacy to go on, and donating your big heart was the best way I could think of to do that. I thought you'd be happy about it."

His shoulders sag. "You gave up so soon. I might've had a chance to come back."

I repeat that and Dr. Latimer shakes his head. "There was no chance you would revive. Your brain was dead and only life-support kept you breathing."

Ralph barely glances at him. "I don't know what happened. I don't remember the accident."

I tell Lori what he's said and she stares at a space not far from where he is. Maybe she can at least sense his energy. "You were out on that stupid motorcycle. I know you felt free riding it, but I told you to be careful. You should've worn a helmet."

He chuckles but brightens. "I died riding my baby? At least I went out happy." He floats around, seeming to be thinking it over. "I had so many plans. So many things I wanted to do."

The Hatches squirm. I quickly tell Lori what he said, and then speak to Ralph again. "Your organs saved this man's life." I point to Mr. Hatch. "One he can now spend with his children. He has four kids. That's the best legacy I can imagine. You live on in a way, and your spirit does, too."

"I can't thank you enough," Mr. Hatch says, and his wife nods enthusiastically. "I get to be a father to my girls, and I promise you, I'm going to be the best dad they could ever have."

Ralph finally agrees it's a good thing. "Does this mean I'll never see my family again?" he asks me.

Persephone steps forward at that point, drawing his attention. "You can visit whenever you want as a spirit guide. Your sister will know you're present, trust me."

He looks at Lori. "Tell her I wish I could hug her one more time."

I relay the message and Lori breaks down crying. Mrs. Hatch pats her back. "I wish that, too," Lori says. "I'll light a candle for you every day, but I'm selling that damn bike."

We all chuckle, including Ralph. "Remind her of our song," he says to me. "I'll make sure she hears it on a regular basis so she doesn't forget me."

"I'll never forget you, moron," she replies when I tell her. "Go enjoy heaven. You better be waiting for me when it's my time to get there."

"You know I will, sis." He blows her a kiss.

Using Winter's technique, I envision a doorway of light and direct him to it. When it's all said and done, everyone seems relieved, and the ghost has crossed over.

I receive handshakes, back pats, and thank-yous as the crowd leaves. Lia chats nonstop about the experience, and begs me to allow her to put it on her vlog.

"We must respect the dead," I tell her. "I know ghosts are a fascinating subject, but we need to remember they were once human beings. I've got a better idea for you."

Her face had fallen, but now lights up. We ascend the stairs. "I get to interview you?"

"How about a guardian angel?" I ask.

Persephone whirls around and glares at me. "Don't even think about it."

As Lia and I leave the hospital, Persephone complaining all the way, I can't keep the grin off my face. "Persephone is such a delight," I tell Lia. "She'll be happy to answer any questions you have."

The girl practically skips to the car. "Omg, I can't wait! I have so many!"

"Ha, ha," Persephone says, floating into the backseat. Sherlock is with her, and he's already tried to convince her this is a great idea. I have the feeling he might like to be interviewed, too. "You're just getting back at me for all the times I haven't been able to tell you what you want to know," she growls.

I glance at her in the rearview as we head down the hill to the street. "Oh yes," I tell Lia with a cheeky grin, "Persephone can hardly wait, either."

My spirit guide makes a gesture that seems completely inappropriate for an angel, but I laugh. Lia is right, being weird is better than being normal.

At the house, I send Lia to the guest room—she's becoming a part of our family, it seems—and start to head upstairs myself. Logan grins and says, "Come closer. Zultan has a message for you."

"Not that again," I say, but something in his eyes lets me know this actually has nothing to do with the fortune teller. Moxley wags his tail as Logan hands me a glass of wine and leads me to the couch. "Have a seat."

I accept the wine. "What's up?"

"Judge Barlow recently purchased a private resort off the coast of Florida. The facility closed a while back, which is how he could afford to buy the whole island, but the main house is still staffed. He's offered it to us to use, free of charge, as a wedding gift."

"I thought we were going to do something big after St. Helen's shindig."

"We are, but you need a break *now*. We both do. A few days away from work and family won't hurt either of us and Rosie and Jenn will handle your business. I've already spoken to them." He hands me a square card with his handwriting on it. "What do you think?"

Sun, sand, and no ghosts, it reads, *are in your future.*

I smile. There are *always* ghosts, but maybe a vacation is a good idea. How many earthbound spirits could be on a private island anyway? "I love the idea."

"You do?"

His happiness is what matters most to me. "I most certainly do." Hopefully, Gloria can finish my trousseau, and maybe it will be the perfect time to bring up my new interest in motherhood with Logan. "A few days on an island with folks waiting on us? Sounds like heaven."

He pulls me into his arms and kisses me. "I'll buy the plane tickets tomorrow."

Persephone appears and she's laughing hysterically. "No ghosts! Ha!"

She disappears just as quickly and I force my lips to keep smiling. "It's going to be great."

"I love you," he says, kissing me again. "It will be nice to have you all to myself for a few days, ghost-free. That will really feel like a honeymoon."

Moxley gives a bark, as if he agrees. Tabby pads into the room, and I swear she has a smile on her feline face.

I down my wine in two gulps. "Yep, ghost-free." I cross my fingers and pray I'll catch a break. "I can't wait."

Don't miss Ava and Logan in Haunted Honeymoon, Confessions of a Closet Medium, an exclusive short story, coming February 2023!

READY FOR MORE MAGICK?

Don't miss the next exciting adventure! Sign up for Nyx's Cozy Clues Mystery Newsletter.

And check out these magical stories:

Sister Witches Of Raven Falls Mystery Series

Sister Witches of Raven Falls Special Collection
Of Potions and Portents
Of Curses and Charms
Of Stars and Spells
Of Spirits and Superstition

Confessions of a Closet Medium Cozy Mystery Series

Confessions of a Closet Medium Special Collection
Pumpkins & Poltergeists
Magic & Mistletoe
Hearts & Haunts

Vows & Vengeance
Cupcakes & Corpses
Tea Leaves & Troubled Spirits (September 2022)

Sister Witches of Story Cove (Formerly Once Upon a Witch) Cozy Mystery Series

Cinder
Belle
Snow
Ruby
Zelle

ABOUT THE AUTHOR

USA Today Bestselling Author Nyx Halliwell grew up on TV shows like *Buffy the Vampire Slayer* and *Charmed.*

She loves writing stories as much as she loves baking and crafting, and believes in magick. We each carry it inside us.

She enjoys binge-watching mystery shows with her hubby and reading all types of stories involving magic and animals.

Connect with Nyx today and see pictures of her pets, be the first to know about new books and sales, and find out when Godfrey, the talking cat, has a new blog post! Receive a FREE copy of the Whitethorne Book of Spells and Recipes by signing up for her newsletter http://eepurl.com/gwKHB9

CONNECT WITH NYX TODAY!

Website: nyxhalliwell.com

Email: nyxhalliwellauthor@gmail.com
Bookbub https://www.bookbub.com/profile/nyx-halliwell
Amazon amazon.com/author/nyxhalliwell
Facebook: https://www.facebook.com/
NyxHalliwellAuthor/

Sign up for Nyx's Cozy Clues Mystery Newsletter and be the FIRST to learn about new releases, sales, behind-the-scenes trivia about the book characters, pictures of Nyx's pets, and links to insightful and often hilarious *From the Cauldron With Godfrey blog*!

DEAR MAGICAL READER

I hope you enjoyed this story! If you did, and would be so kind, would you leave a review on Goodreads, Book-bub, or your favorite book retailer? I would REALLY appreciate it!

A review lets hundreds, if not thousands, of potential readers know what you enjoyed about the book, and helps them make wise buying choices. It's the best word-of-mouth around.

The review doesn't have to be anything long! Pretend you're sharing the story with a good friend. Pick out one or more characters, scenes, or dialogue that made you smile, laugh, or warmed your heart, and tell them about it. Just a few sentences is perfect!

Blessed be,

Nyx 🤍

CPSIA information can be obtained
at www.ICGtesting.com
Printed in the USA
LVHW082143261022
731683LV00032B/915